I0841033

Bad Agency

Bad Agency
The Residue of Trauma

Irina Ember

Cover art and layout: Morphos Inc.
Typesetting: Iñaki Fernández de Retana.

Bad Agency is a work of fiction. Names, characters, places, and incidents are either products of the author's imagination or are used fictitiously. Any resemblance to actual persons, living or dead, events or locals are entirely coincidental.

ISBN
9798218172145 paperback

Dedicated to my friend and teacher,
the late, great Dale Hoyt.

Acknowledgements

Thank you to Nancy Fish for all the help and referrals to great people and resources. Thank you to Iñaki Fernández de Retana for the editing and also the encouragement. Thank you to Gregg Sugerman for the coaching, the support, and for believing in me. Thank you to Gabrielle Thormann for reading and for the feedback and suggestions. Thank you to SG Browne, Matthew A. Goodwin, Debra Olivier, and David Shields, all published authors who have been generous with their advice. A big thank you to April Eberhardt for reading and giving me feedback and advice.

IT'S HARD TO LIVE IN THE WORLD AS A TRAUMA SURVIVOR. You can't think about your trauma all the time because you won't be able to function but you can't forget it either. It seeps out from behind your eyes, escapes from your ears like steam, and leaves a trace like greasy fingers do. Trauma creates an energy field of shame, mine does anyway, and I just have to fake it every day, pretend that I feel okay despite having convinced myself that I am to blame for what happened to me—all of it. And there's so much. Like a snowball going downhill, my trauma compounds itself and attracts the newly fallen trauma along the way. At first, it seems light and fluffy and harmless but eventually, it becomes one with this deadly, icy ball. It's still not as much as some others have been through though, and I feel sorry for them too. Of course, there are days I mostly forget, and it just bubbles under the surface, a delirious, repetitive soundtrack to my life.

When you pretend for long enough and you see that you pass, you start to believe your own deception despite being a broken vessel. But when there is too much pressure, the cracks start to show. There are the sometimes random, sometimes triggered flashbacks: pictures, sensations, combinations of images and feelings that convey some well-worn meaning, such as: There's something wrong with me. Or: I am alone. Or: Something bad is going to happen. It's a rotating menu of negative feelings. There's a passively accessed catalog of still images from scary events; there have been so many. My body is riveted by a cellular change activated by the most primal part of my brain. I'm not conscious of it and I can't breathe it away or think it away. A hot shower might help, but I'm not normally in my shower when triggered.

Between attacks, I'm like an octopus in shallow water with the pull of the tide moving me over the sand and rocks. I am interrupted by sensations, as though a piece of fabric is brushing against my skin, or I am walking through a cloud of gas, random as a spirit in an old house. Or a sea shanty runs through my head and my teeth and my fingers, tapping itself out in a neurotic pattern that will not relent until my jaw is tight. Shallow breathing.

At times of peace, I feel as though I am a welded vessel with magic dust inside, creating music and triggering random eruptions in some dislocated inner area where my emotions are born. I am always checking for the possibility of another attack. Why do I ruminate so much? Is it to remind me of my story so that I never live it again? For as long as I continue to retrace the trauma, it remains entrenched, a wired connection in my brain, a shortcut to the emotional seizure or a dis-associated state if the pain is too strong. It seems I don't want to change. Why would I? My story is who I am, what I am. How else will I know myself?

It's hard to recall the past when the brain's ability to record events has been damaged. What I do know is that a listing ship can right itself in a storm, even with a tattered sail and a broken mast. It does happen if the conditions are right. I am one of the lucky ones. I know I can pass. That's why some of these real estate people are so confused about my bad attitude and why I'm not selling more real estate. It's because my life is leaky. I've been trying to stay in the present world while the traces of my trauma follow me everywhere. Shrapnel. A life exploded.

Chapter 1
Ruby Gets Dressed

2019. I WOKE UP AT 5 AM. IT WAS COLD. I used the battery-powered remote to turn on the gas fireplace. *Thank goodness for gas.* I had hot water as well from the gas-fired water heater, just no electricity. All the ice had melted in the freezer, and there was a puddle on the floor, which I cleaned in the darkness.

It was the beginning of summer, and the fires were burning again. I hypnotized myself every day by staring at the news on my phone until it seemed like it was happening somewhere else, to somebody else, but the smoke in the dark was so eerie that it was hard not to feel a deep terror. *How will I escape if the fire comes?* I knew everybody would jump in their minivans at the last minute and render the escape route a parking lot of death. I imagined driving the wrong way down the roads, forcing the two-way street to become a double-wide one-way. *Should I get a motor scooter so that I can split lanes with my cat meowling in her carrier, strapped to the back seat? We should be rehearsing this. We should be practicing evacuations now before we are all so panicked that we can't think straight and we are forced to die in our cars, skeletons still seated in the smoking remains of our melted metal carriages. This life has been so long, and I'm ready to be at peace but I prefer not to be burned alive with my cat and all my cheap belongings.*

I got dressed early and drove to San Francisco while tiny bits of ash were falling on the windshield before a dirty orange sky. I was wearing kitten heels. *Ridiculous.*

Chapter 2
Ready to Rumble

IN THE CITY, THE STREETS WERE JAMMED WITH CARS. Some bicyclist in the lane next to me mistook me for a different driver in a similar car and raged at me. When I shrugged in what I thought was a gesture of solidarity with him, he spit in my passenger-side window, which was open just a fist. My upper body began trembling violently as I lay on my horn and shouted out the window, "Spitting is assault!" multiple times until other drivers and pedestrians were craning their necks to see the crazy lady.

I knew how it looked: a dressed-up, middle-aged lady raging behind the wheel of a Mercedes. I felt the shame, the self-accusations creeping over me like a shroud as I hunched over the steering wheel in my car, hoping to be invisible as I drove away, the watching public's imagined narrative about me already internalized: *I have no right to complain about the pain inside my head, my body, my soul. So many people in this world have real suffering that is much worse than mine.*

A half-mile away, I parked next to a village of sidewalk tent-dwellers, stepped over some discarded clothing and trash amid the urine smell, and fed the meter. San Francisco's normally cold in the summer, but today it already felt like the sidewalk was melting. I was still triggered, and emotional pain had flooded my body so that I walked with a sort of a

limp because of the sudden void of endorphins or whatever
was chemically going on after the altercation with the angry
cyclist. I glanced at the young guy seated at the edge of the
tent city. He had a giant, lumpy brown dog with its sad face
resting on its paws. The dog looked like his owner, resigned
and beaten down. The owner looked upset like he was under
the full assault of his own mind. It seemed obvious to me that
he had been abused as a child, like that girl at the psychiatric
institute who told me she had endured beatings by her reli-
gious mother until she saw the Angel Gabriel. I met her the
third and last time I was institutionalized, at age eighteen.

I never thought I was too scary of a crazy person back then,
but I wasn't exactly safe either, and I was absolutely a danger to myself. I had nowhere to stay when I arrived by bus
in New York. I slept in the bus station the first night because
it seemed like the right place to be when you are homeless,
but I didn't get any sleep. I was suffering emotionally as one
dangerous event followed another in what seemed like a
dislocated timeline. I gave away my jacket when I stayed in
the Covenant House because I was scared of the other girls.
I went home with a strange man who tried to get rid of me
once he realized I was psychotic and wouldn't uncurl from
a fetal position after we smoked marijuana. I accidentally
set a sofa on fire and stole a bunch of coins from a nice lady
who let me stay at her place while she was out of town. I
couldn't keep a job because the register could never be rec-
onciled. They thought I was stealing. I went into a time warp
while serving donuts and coffee at a fast-food chain and was
unable to tell at what speed I was moving. I made art out of
garbage and tried to sell it on the street, figuring I was probably an artist since I had lost my mind.

At least I knew I had lost my mind. Some people don't know.

Actually, after having hitchhiked home from New York
City, I did try to act scary by hiding a knife in my sleeve
at my mom's house while I was talking to her, bedside,
after being summoned upstairs. That was the last time I
ever stayed at her house because she made me stay in the

basement like I was a stranger and somebody she mistrusted. Like I wasn't even family. It wasn't my intention to do anything. She was treating me like I was a sick person, and I was responding in kind, holding the knife mostly hidden in my sleeve as I went to her. I was playing a role that she had assigned me. I was giving her what she wanted, what she was projecting onto me—probably her own homicidal rage, but my brains were too scrambled at that point to recognize it. I just wanted her to stop abusing me. But even that didn't make her stop. She would never stop. She looked up at me from her bed and told me she understood if I "had to go," which I took to mean "go ahead and kill yourself like your sister." She probably could have caused me to turn that knife on myself because there I was like a dummy, a braindead junky, still hoping she was going to love me, yearning to get what I was never given: just a small drop of unconditional love and acceptance. Even just a relenting of the harassment and manipulation and humiliation that I had endured by her and that was now internalized. That would have been some relief.

I called the paramedics and told them I was thinking of cutting myself in the neck with that knife and that I was thinking they could come to take some blood from me instead so that the pressure would stop, the pressure inside my head and body. They did come but only to take me away while all the neighbors gawked from their driveways. It's been more than twenty-five years since I lost it, but you don't ever really come back from that, not completely.

I wobbled in my heels three blocks to the office and waited in the lobby for the incredibly slow elevator, depressed about my life, dreading having to show my face, but still determined to make something of myself, or at least figure out how to be financially stable. That's one of the characteristics that helps me survive as a real estate agent: persistence. I used to want to be an artist, a musician, or a writer but I wasn't good enough or sane enough to be any of those things and I got tired of pretending it was stylish to be poor. Now I'm one hundred percent commission, and my income goes up, it goes back down, and I hustle and hustle, introducing myself to people I don't know at open houses, trying to get them to give me their email addresses so that I can send them online listings that they increasingly prefer to find on their own. I would probably do better if I wasn't embarrassed about my profession. The agents in my office seem proud to have chosen this career, maybe because they are making so much money. *I need to figure out how to do those big deals.* I leaned into the elevator button again.

Chapter 3
Love in an Elevator

THE ELEVATOR FINALLY ARRIVED. I could hear that somebody else had entered the lobby but I kept my head down and tried to close the doors so I wouldn't have to share the ride. A giant hand reached into my peripheral view.

"You're not trying to leave without me, are you?"

It was Adrian. He smiled and spread his arms out, making a hug inescapable. He was maybe twelve years my junior—six feet of strong, confident, cocky man with caramel skin, broad shoulders, and bulging arm muscles—and a snappy dresser. Charming. He smelled so good, and it felt nice to be in his embrace, but I was shy. He was too good-looking.

Before we hooked up last year, we had flirted hard at an office party, then sent a thousand horny text messages and emails back and forth, finally setting a date for a Saturday. In person, his seduction was intense, captivating, skilled, and charismatic, but via email, it was drawn out for too long, and I became bored of it, knowing that he probably wouldn't deliver the goods he was promising. I figured I could show him the way since I knew I must have more experience than he and I daydreamed about it to keep myself interested until the actualization of our rendezvous.

The first time, we did it in my bed, and it was good, but he hurt me because he was so strong and he manhandled me.

He was way ahead and totally in charge, undressing me and kissing me and maneuvering my body and putting a condom on and sliding the giant thing into me. I had to rush ahead in my mind to keep up with him, trying to get something out of it before he finished. I acted like I was enjoying it, making the noises, tossing my hair, trying to look attractive and distract him from noticing my sagging skin, my lumpy places, my stretch marks, my wrinkles. He was beautiful, with the long, lean, muscular body that some surfers have. He was young, and his skin was soft from a layer of light downy hair. I felt like a monster in comparison to him, sweaty, bumpy, uneven, and imperfect—it made me so nervous that I took no action toward my goal of showing him how I could be sensual and skilled in bed. Suddenly, he jammed my body against his, forcing me to orgasm, which wasn't what I wanted at that moment. I had imagined being in control of my own desire and his, but I wasn't able to do it. My own desire was trapped inside my head while I intuited, internalized, and shadowed his.

When it was over and he went home, I noticed I was bruised and sore. Suddenly, he came back and knocked on my door because, he said, he had left his sunglasses. I had been relaxing and really wanted to lay around alone and recover from the sex but I let him in, and one thing led to another. We went to my bedroom again. The tone had changed for some reason, and he acted nastier than before.

"Ow, ow, ow, ow," I recited with every thrust, not even trying to act like I was enjoying it this time. He pounded away regardless of my whimpers. He choked me, grabbed my hair, and pulled it and was doing it wrong, not the way I liked it. I didn't want to interrupt his enjoyment of my body or embarrass him by letting him know he wasn't pleasing me, even though I was concerned he might pull some of my hair out. The more I accommodated him, the more pleasure he seemed to gain from it, as evidenced by his moans and his slapping me like a slow horse. I started to think he was stupid for not knowing that I was in pain, even though I still did not say anything. I was embarrassed for him. Didn't know or didn't care? Wouldn't any intelligent being recognize the sound of an animal suffering and stop to make sure the animal is okay?

Intellectually, I know it hurts me to do things that I do not want to do and to pretend that I like doing those things but I can't stop, and when it happens, I feel that I am being suffocated, buried alive. More than thirty years have passed since my mother terrorized me, and I'm still disassociated from myself, from my being, like a ghost. I don't know how to find my own feelings. How does he feel, what does he want, what does he think of me: these thoughts are my preoccupation while little me is lost, captive in the basement of my childhood.

When he was finally done, I draped my arm across his chest and smiled, assuming he learned his bad habits from watching the misogynist internet porn that is ubiquitous these days; he didn't know any better. I decided to be grateful—even if Adrian choked and bruised me and then wasn't able to make a subsequent date with me, I was glad to be having sex with such a beautiful young man. In fact, I felt like I was supposed to brag about sex with a hot guy the way the boys used to about girls who they had determined to be hot back in high school. It seemed like they were hunting us girls back then, isolating us from the herd and going in for the kill. Of course, I was already the sick animal on the edges that was easy to spot and pick off. My family was so abnormal that I grew up defenseless, more than defenseless. I walked myself into each situation intentionally, every time more dangerous than the one before: the angry boyfriend trying to force himself on his girlfriend, the tenth grader seducing the naïve freshman at school, the preppy in the bar hitting on the underage girl dressed like an escort, the stoner at the party luring in the lost girl, the rapist pretending to be the helpful cab driver, the guy on the corner who just attacks and doesn't pretend to be nice, the friendly area pimp.

"That was the best ev-ah," Adrian had said afterward in some sort of vernacular.

I had flashed back to all that while Adrian stood smiling at me.

"Everything good?"

"Good. Yes. Good. Hope you're doing some deals."

"Nice to see you." He hugged me again, smiling, and went on his way. I headed out of the elevator toward reception.

Chapter 4
The Bathroom

I WALKED PAST THE ENTRY AREA AND GLANCED ACROSS the main floor of the office where the weekly meetings are held. Empty. Just an expanse with muted sun from the sky-light three floors above. Two giant copiers were at the other end of the room where a penitent transaction coordinator waddled to the copier and stared listlessly at the machine as it spit out paper. I always prefer to be at the office when it is empty, but it is a stressful and depressing place regardless; soon enough, there would be throngs of agents milling about, making mindless conversation with one another. The private offices for "top" agents who could afford to pay extra were spread out in a ring around the lobby, so it was hard to tell how many people were actually in the office at any given time. The upper floors had the same layout, minus the lobby but plus a catwalk that allowed you to peer over the rail to the lobby floor below—a stage with a built-in spotlight.

This office was way better than my last one at the low-end brokerage, which had cheap walls taped together in a tiny space, a real mouse habitat where you could hear the other desperate agents in their partitioned areas trying to coerce their clients into signing contracts. This fancy office was fully remodeled in a prestigious Nob Hill location. The main level had a mini kitchen with an endless supply of tea and coffee drinks. On the upper level, there was a full kitchen for the staff where people would microwave the weird food they brought from home and talk candidly without the interruption of having to accommodate demanding agents and their clients. Agents are the pushiest people in the world, always trying to make something happen, even if it's something as unmanageable as the weather. They can't help but try. I suppose I am the same way but I believe I'm different than the worst agents; I try not to actively destroy other people who are in the process of getting in my way. But treating people well in this business just makes you seem weak to the mean agents.

I pushed open the door to the first-floor women's bathroom and went into the one empty toilet enclosure. The other two doors were closed. There was somebody in the stall next to me, and I heard what sounded like a weak fart. Somebody left the other stall as two more ladies came into the bathroom, their heels clicking on the tile floor, chatting as they stood by the sinks and sitting area. I tried to pee silently.

"And they put a lock box on it but just left the door open. I mean, they were living there."

"Weird."

"I know. Out-of-town agent. I think she was from Marin or something."

"I don't think she does any deals."

"She doesn't know how to negotiate at our level, that's for sure."

"Well, not everybody can be Ivy League in this business."

"They should make a rule about it!"

They both laughed. *What elitist bitches,* I thought, hating that I was one of these people.

The person next to me seemed to be trying to wait out the new visitors. I left my stall, went to the sink, and glanced at the petite woman closest to me as she headed toward the exit. She kept her head down even though we have spoken to one another in the past. She looked mousy, drab, and unexceptional, yet carried herself in a way that seemed arrogant. I've noticed her in meetings in the past because her voice is grating, and she sounds so self-important when she speaks.

The other woman and I looked at each other. It was Ugly-Jacket Lady, an older monster agent, as in monster truck, as in big, as in selling a ton of very expensive properties.

"Hi, how are you," I said as a greeting but not an actual question. I felt dead inside.

"How are you doing?" she asked with false interest. She probably couldn't remember my name, but I'm sure she remembered that I was one of the loser agents who doesn't do much business.

"Me? I'm fine. How are you?"

"Nice hair," she told me.

"Nice outfit," I replied. "You're so coordinated. Even your glasses—they're so trippy."

I knew it was a stupid thing to say as soon as the words came out but I also knew this lady was so focused on her own agenda that it would have no consequence. She was wearing a silk top and skirt that had some garish, matching pattern like the bomber jacket thing that she had been wearing that other time. Today's outfit looked like a sofa and matching drapes in silk, name brand. I figured she had walked into some designer store and bought whatever they told her to buy then matched her nail color and lipstick to the outfit. She looked like a child who had been dressed by a parent to make a big impression on the first day of school or win a career as a child star in Hollywood, except her face looked old as dust.

She peered at me sideways out of one eye like a bird at a worm, her swollen eye bags and sagging, grey flesh magnified by her giant, pink-framed eyeglasses.

"I need an extra helper this weekend. Are you available for open houses?"

"Yes, I'm available, what do you have?" You have to watch out for agents who use you and stick you on a dead listing where you can't pick up any leads.

"Oh, I have this fabulous loft," she gushed. "Striking custom artwork, very stylish." She looked at me smugly.

"I'm available," I said without hesitation. "Let me know what day." I felt like I had to grab it before she offered it to some other desperate agent. I should have asked her about the activity level before accepting but I didn't have anything else lined up. I'm sure she guessed as much.

"Sunday, one to three or two to four, your choice." She acted as though she was doing me a giant favor by giving me the open.

"I'll do two to four. Thank you for thinking of me. I'll give you a full report," I said, trying to impress her with my thorough nature and strong work ethic.

"And you can try being enthusiastic…"

"Oh. Do I not sound enthusiastic?" I noticed that I sounded less human than a robot. I tried not to react to the criticism. I know I have a flat affect but I didn't think I was expected to sound all perky while in a bathroom agreeing to do another agent's open house for free.

"No." She stared at me with no expression. It was confrontational.

"Oh, uh, well, I mean…I will cover all the selling points," I stammered. She had me on the defensive.

She looked down her nose at me. "I'll have my assistant send you the details."

"Okay…" I said, indicating I wasn't really pleased with her, which seemed to make her happy. She gave me a cursory smile then sashayed into the empty stall. *What a fucking freak!*

I walked away from Ugly-Jacket Lady and exited the restroom. I thought I had held my ground but realized I felt like an alien observer, dysregulated out of my body again, my thoughts raging. I'm knocked off balance so easily. I solicited this life, but the office was just another place I didn't want to be. *I'm not like these people.*

THE SECOND TIME I WAS SENT AWAY, it was to a bizarre institution called, The Farm Place. It was the middle of winter in Connecticut, and I didn't stay long. The patients there were just too crazy compared to me. I was out of my mind but I knew I didn't belong there with folks who thought they were witches or said they had taken so much LSD that they had talked to God multiple times. I mean, I did entertain the possibility that I could leave the earth with my body but I also thought of it as a metaphor, and I knew it was a weird thought that I might not want to share with other people. If I ever thought I was like Jesus or something, I knew I wasn't actually Jesus. I was grieving, suicidal, and disassociated, plus I had smoked PCP, which hurried me along the road toward psychosis as well as a strange detachment from my physical sensations.

I told the staff I was leaving, and they said, okay, we can't stop you but we have to call your dad. They put me on the phone with him, and he said that he would have to send the police after me, and I said: do what you have to do. I wasn't a criminal. I left there with a loaf of bread and a couple of pieces of fruit, plus my bag of vintage coats that I scored at the flea market in Amsterdam back when my dad had sent me to Europe after my sister died. I cared what I wore even though I was walking devastation; I spun my sorrow and illness into something tragically romantic in my head. I slept in the woods, finding pine needles to make a soft bed and piling my coats on top of me. I found berries and I collected them, thinking they might be poison. I ate them and dreamed strange things but did not die, my sleep fitful and broken by the incessant barking of a nearby dog.

I woke in the morning to realize I was not in the woods, just a rural patch of trees next to a road that led to the highway. I walked to the onramp and held my thumb out to catch a ride. I was out of place hitchhiking in rural Connecticut in the winter: an eighteen-year-old, overweight, goth female with chopped-off hair and a vintage leather coat and army duffel bag. Some old lady with blond hair drove by, sunken in her seat like a shriveled apple, avoiding any eye contact

even though we were the only two humans visible to the
horizon. Then a guy named Barry came and gave me a
ride to the bus station and some money to take the bus. He
helped me and did not murder me or try to have sex with me.
He was kind, and when I offered to repay him, he said don't
worry about it and that I could do the same for somebody
else someday. His kindness toward a stranger still makes me
cry. I thought right then that if I ever could help somebody
that way, I would.

Chapter 5

A Generous Attempt to Appear to Be Helpful

I WANDERED TOWARD THE MAIL SLOTS AND PEEKED INTO MINE, hoping to see something that looked like a check. Nothing. Just returned marketing postcards and real estate agent junk mail. The big agents get their commissions wired into their accounts but they haven't approved me for that, so I have to come in physically to check my mailbox every single day that I am expecting a check.

"Hi Allie," I said to our receptionist as I marched myself over to the front desk. Allie was standing behind the marble, U-shaped vestibule wearing skin-tight black pants that could have been leggings except that they seemed to have metal zippers across each hip. I wasn't sure if they were real zippers or if that was just decoration. *I have no idea what's happening with fashion.*

When I saw her shoes, my eyes almost popped out of my head, they were so inappropriate in the real estate office setting. She was wearing sexy, patent-leather stiletto heels with peek-a-boo holes showing her bright red toenails crammed together. Her boobs were jammed high up on her chest, and her moderate cleavage was threatening to heave out of her shimmery black top. She was both skinny and curvaceous. I tried not to stare. I felt old and dumpy.

"Oh, hi Ruby." Allie glanced at me for just a moment, and I noticed her cat eyeliner and smooth forehead: bored or at least completely unworried, plus the heavy eyelids of a stoner. She was doing busy work that the front desk person is required to do, logging package arrivals into the manifest, delivering mail, leaving keys for agents to pick up when deals closed, and filling the bowl with mints. I took a handful of mints and shoved them in my pocket when she wasn't looking.

"Hey, do you know if a check came in for me today? I finally had a tiny deal close."

"No, nothing came in for you yet today."

"Oh, drag," I lamented. "Okay, I'll check back. Drat." Allie didn't look up. "Everything okay?" I asked her. She glanced at me and hesitated.

"Oh…can I tell you something?" She went back to looking down, her cat-like eyes a little bit crossed.

"Sure, what's going on?"

"Bryce told me I look sexy."

I was stunned and had to examine in my head what she had just said to be sure I was correctly hearing and interpreting it.

"Oh, uh-oh." I stammered. She was silent. Bryce was the perfect-hair, silver-spoon, country-club, fratty vice-president of the brokerage. This was not good. "Oh, jeez. Do you want me to say something to Charlene about it?" Charlene was the secondary sales manager/office manager/glorified admin, a real deadbeat and not somebody I really wanted to have to approach, but at least she was a woman, somebody who should back up our receptionist's right to not have suggestive comments made to her by her employer and superior while she is at work. "I'll ask her to say something, but I won't mention your name. Do you want me to do that?"

"Yes," she said. I was surprised by how quickly she replied.

"Okay. I'll take care of it. I'm sorry about that. That's not okay," I blurted, unable to be as cool as the young receptionist. She seemed a little bit relieved. I'm an independent contractor, and I don't think we are by law afforded any sort of protection from other creepy agents or the managers hitting on us, but I knew the employees had rights. Poor Allie.

Why would Bryce be so dumb as to say something like that to an employee? It's true that Allie on the daily dresses inappropriately, in my opinion, but I would never say anything to her about that. She did usually look like a slinky model to me. One time I saw her at the office in what looked like actual lingerie: a shorts and camisole set with stockings and heels. I nearly laughed when I saw it because it made me think of the word *boudoir*. It was so wildly inappropriate and unlike what any person would wear to work in an office. But just before I had blurted out, "nice outfit," I jammed my lips closed and realized it was none of my business how she dressed.

She had barely looked at me during the time I was standing there talking to her, and she was already starting to go back to her desk duties.

"Okay, I will take care of it," I told her. "I'm so sorry that happened," I repeated, backing away from her. I felt like a hero, offering to take it up with somebody on her behalf even though I can't ever stand up or advocate for myself.

Chapter 6
The Menace of the Office Manager

NORMALLY THE OFFICE MANAGER at a real estate brokerage is there to help agents with their deals, but
no-neck Charlene just hangs around in her boxy
yellow dress trying to get deals from the agents. She teaches
the Monday night real estate class for the newer agents,
waddling back and forth in front of the students, repeating
her mantra like a cult leader.

"*Remember…when* you get a client who wants to do a
deal…*I'm* your person. Bring it to me, and I'll help you
list it or I'll help you with your buyer. Bring it right to me.
I will help you get that listing and I will help you write that
contract."

It works too; new and loner agents bring her deals they
don't think they can handle on their own. So, she gets paid
a salary to manage the office and she's also picking up deals
from new agents who don't understand that what she's really
doing is skimming. It's a giant conflict of interest since she is
supposed to be there to help the agents succeed. She's a toad
sitting around catching flies.

I knocked on the glass door frame, and it made a weird
bonking noise. She was inside hunched over her desk, staring
at a screen, and didn't look at me or say anything. I took one
small step inside her office.

"Hello?" Still nothing. "Um, Charlene? I have something I need to discuss?" I sounded so wimpy and uncertain trying not to bother her. She still said nothing and only moved her eyes toward me. "Can I discuss something with you?"

"What." She didn't even make it sound like a question and returned her eyes to the screen.

"Um, one of our employees has had an issue with management. I think somebody said something inappropriate to her."

"What do you want me to do about it?"

"Uh, handle the complaint?" Nothing. "Are you the person I should take this to?"

"Bryce."

"Oh…I have to take this to Bryce?" For some reason, I couldn't tell her that this was about Bryce. "Um, but I think it's something that could be construed as sexual harassment, and I was thinking it might be better to have a female handle it for sensitivity reasons. Of course, I don't know the protocol."

"Bryce."

"Oh, uh, because I don't know if he is really going to be the right person to take this to. Are you sure?"

She looked at me like I was stupid, letting it sink in, apparently unwilling to help. I backed out into the hall. *She's such a horrible human being.* I was mad at myself for letting Charlene get to me. My every interaction with her made me feel powerless, and this time was no exception. I felt ineffectual and small and considerably less vigilant.

I made it halfway down the hall and found Bryce's big chest suddenly impeding my path.

"Ruby! How's my favorite agent?" He was all smiles, a thousand feet of the whitest teeth around.

"Oh, uh, I'll let you know if I run into them." I rolled my eyes in a lame attempt at a joke that I presumed he would not find funny. For how jolly he is, I have never found Bryce to have an actual sense of humor.

"That's the attitude!" He moved beside me and put his arm around my shoulders. I looked up at his face. I had no idea whether he had missed my joke or if he was just disregarding it. At such close proximity, his features looked too small, and I wondered if he had his nose done. The nostrils were too tiny and perfect, yet not even with each other.

"Ruby, I've been thinking about you! How's business? Lay it on me."

I had no idea what to say. I have always been impressed by Bryce, by his physical size and appearance, which is always immaculate, from his coiffed hair to his Brooks Brothers suit and silk tie to his Bentley. He was fancy. And so positive—friendly, chipper, encouraging. It took me so many failed conversations with him to come up with a word to explain why I never clicked with him: "phony." There was something that just wasn't quite right, but for the life of me, I couldn't put my finger on it. I knew some of it might be me. Most of the time, I'm trying to fix myself because I think there's some-thing wrong with me. I'm on a lifetime journey to figure out what it is but, in the meantime, I still have to make a living, I still have goals, I still have to make my way in the world like everybody else. I try to hide my repulsive self-loathing as I present a sheen of confidence scraped up from the tiniest vestiges of positive self-regard that I find in my inherent intel-ligence. I know I am smart.

A difference between Bryce and me is I feel like everybody can see through my veneer since I can see through theirs. I know it's so obvious that I'm faking it every day. Not Bryce. He believes his personal propaganda, and I can't see past his veneer. He's like a giant, walking, talking cardboard cutout of a person. He doesn't seem all that bright to me, so deep down, I feel I am better than him yet I suspect he views me as a pathetic loser, and I also sympathize with his point of view. He is positive and encouraging to me like he is with every-body, but I just don't think it's for real.

"I'm here for you, Ruby. I think you're not performing at your potential, am I right?" An agent walked toward us down the hall, and Bryce moved me out of the way by placing his hand on the small of my back. I acted like I didn't notice, even though it made me feel uncomfortable.

"Oh, god, okay, is that what we're doing right now?"
I should have kept that as a thought in my head. But I did
say it out loud. "I mean, yes, obviously, I should be doing
more business than I am doing," I stammered, trying to sound
hopeful. I didn't understand why Bryce was suddenly so
interested in helping me.

"I agree! You look the part—so what's going on?"

"I mean, I'm doing everything. I took the coaching class.
I do the open houses. I send out the postcards." I could hear
myself sounding whiney.

"And is that working for you?"

"No." I tried to think of something positive to say so that he
wouldn't tell me that I was to blame for my own lack of success. "I'm a good agent."

"Oh, I'm sure of that. You wouldn't be here otherwise. I've
only heard the best things about you as an agent."

"Oh, really?" I couldn't imagine that to be true.

"I think with a little attitude adjustment, you could do really
well. Are you able to see that?"

I tried not to let my face show the discouragement welling
up in me. *Not this again,* I thought. This is my fourth brokerage, and every single manager or broker I've had so far has
told me, in some manner, that I am too negative. I'm so tired
of guys like this telling me that I just need to change my attitude, be more positive, look on the bright side, whatever.

"What do you think you are getting out of it, Ruby?" They all
ask. They don't understand that it's not so easy for somebody
like me. I can't tell Bryce that, of course, partly because I can't
see clearly what's happening to me but also because I know
he wouldn't understand. *He can't possibly comprehend.*

It's not like I haven't tried. I have been to hundreds of
hours of therapy in my life, starting when I was four years old.
I've tried some meds that worked, but then some doctor told
me I was severely depressed and prescribed some heavier
meds. After I took those and imagined hanging myself with a
belt, I decided that they had no idea how medication works
and quit taking those.

I have done holistic stuff and spiritual stuff and tapping and EMDR and journaling, acupuncture, self-help stuff, affirmations, meditations, hypnosis, and energy healing. So far, it hasn't worked; I'm still broken. I exercise and watch videos and read books and listen to podcasts. I have coaches and bodyworkers, and practically every dollar I make I spend trying to make myself well, trying to heal myself and find out how to be authentic, how to be happy, how to be whole and healthy. I mean, I'm better, slightly, but I still have bad relationships and I still can't stand up for myself. I keep putting myself in harm's way, meaning physical harm, mental harm, spiritual harm, and professional harm. I know this. But a mind can't just be changed like that. Mine seems intractable. And it's all so discouraging, and then of course it doesn't help me because I get down on myself because I can't seem to change, and everybody blames me, and believe me, I also blame myself.

"Why don't you ask Allie to set up a meeting with me?" Bryce touched the small of my back again and then lingered there, which I ignored, even though it made me want to squirm away from him.

"Uh, okay." Inexplicably, I rolled my eyes as though I knew he would never genuinely want to help me. He grimaced in response.

"Did you ever think you are the reason for your own lack of success, Ruby?" He took his hand off my back and pointed to his own head. *Here it comes.* "I think you really have to ask yourself why you are so negative. What are you getting out of it? Take a look at somebody like Katy. She came here with no experience but she has a can-do attitude. And she's cute as a button on top of it! Now she's working with Tab, one of the top performers in our brokerage. If you could get over your attitude, it might help you with your business. You just need to get out of your head."

Ugh, why did he bring up Katy, the slutty-looking preppy from Texas who was probably twenty years my junior? She showed up six months ago and planted herself every day on a stool near the copiers, pretending to have work to do on her laptop while in the common area, wearing cheerleader-type miniskirts with high heels and no stockings, striking up inane conversations with anybody she thought might get her somewhere. She was moderately polite to me but with no enthusiasm behind it, as though she knew we had nothing to barter. I felt an instant wave of aggression rise inside me.

"Some agent told Allie she looked sexy," I blurted out recklessly. He looked into my eyes for a moment and did not blink, then turned his attention to pulling his cuffs out from under his jacket.

"If you don't want to talk about how you can improve your sales, then I don't think I will be able to help you, Ruby." I knew he had heard what I said, and it was clear he did not like hearing it.

He buttoned up his jacket as though he were leaving but recovered quickly. "Did she say that? That doesn't sound like something an agent should say to our receptionist. That's not something anybody should be saying to her. I'll take care of it, Ruby, and thank you for telling me about it. You did the right thing," he said, reaching over and patting my shoulder heavily three times. I knew at that moment I had not done the right thing at all. "Let's set up a meeting next week." He smiled but he looked at me like he thought I was pathetic. "Call Allie this afternoon and tell her that you need to set up a coaching meeting with me, please." He stepped to the side and motioned with his arm for me to walk past him. "Good talk, Ruby."

I regretted saying it. Why couldn't I just fit in like Katy? Why couldn't I just keep my mouth shut and play along, play the game, whatever the fucking game is? Now he probably would view me as a threat to be taken out. Why would he want to help me now? I didn't care about Bryce, not on a personal level, because he could never understand me. Whatever his struggles, whatever he thought he had overcome, it was outside of the comprehension of a life like mine. A disaster of a life like mine. He could never imagine my experiences in life, and I didn't dare tell him. *There's a reason I am the way I am. There's a reason I'm negative—because I can't imagine anything ever working out for me in this life. It never has.* And nothing about any of that will help me sell more real estate.

Chapter 7

The Malaise of the Angry Agent

I DON'T MAKE ENOUGH MONEY TO PAY THE EXTRA FEE for a real office at this brokerage and I'm what's called a "floater agent," relegated to working in the one part of the office that is not upscale, a bit of leftover space on the floor above reception, right in between a major walkway, the elevators, the printer station, the electric shredding machine, and the fancy offices for the top producers. The upside is it's free, but the downside is we have to use one of six desktop computers with phones all jammed together and separated by flimsy partitions behind which you can hear the spit in your neighbor's mouth while they talk on the phone—not such an upgrade from the last rathole I worked in. The glamorous world of real estate.

Some of the floaters hold back from announcing all the details of their lives and deals while in these public offices in the middle of the upper floor; others do not. One droopy lady is always up there with her ragged, mangy dog that comes begging for affection, while she calls after it, "Fluffy, Fluff-eeey, F-l-u-f-f-e-e-y." *Lady, your dog is right here, one cubicle away,* I wanted to say. The dog was always trying too hard, panhandling for affection like an unemployed circus animal.

And the Russian lady agent was in the office today. Sometimes I wanted to punch the divider to get her to stop talking so loudly. I would rustle my computer and bang it on the desktop to make sure she knew somebody else was there. *Why are agents so inconsiderate?* That lady is totally oblivious and also not at all friendly, a terrible combination. I would become angrier and angrier as she droned on about how to price the client's house, why it had to be that price, and what was going on with houses in that same area. I imagined shoving the entirety of the dividers over on top of the lady to get her to stop. *I don't know why or when I became such an angry person. Angry and sad.*

It was afternoon, finally, and Fluffy the dog was staggering around the cubicles like a haggard comedian in Las Vegas, grinning with his dog gums, begging for scraps of affection. I gave him the finger. I had been at the floater station for hours, achieving nothing aside from rumination, when my phone rang.

"Hey girl…"

It was Julie. She was actually a client of mine, having done three deals with me in the past, but we now had some sort of friendship, though I often felt overextended when I spent any time with her.

"What's up?" I said flatly. My flat affect does have different tones, and Julie at least gets it. When she speaks, her intonation always goes down at the end of every sentence as though she is beleaguered by everything she experiences in life.

"Oh, nothing, I'm just working. Are you at work?" She pretty much does data entry from home for a living.

"Yeah, I'm at the office," I said with a hushed tone, trying not to expose every detail of my life to the other losers in my vicinity. The floater desks were also close to a few open offices, and I never knew which nosy agents might be lurking judgmentally.

"What are you doing tonight? Want to go out?"

That was code for did I want to buy her a drink and an appetizer. I used to say yes at the drop of a hat because

I have no social life and she is entertaining, but on our out-
ings, she would regularly circumvent the happy hour menu,
ask to taste wines, order the most expensive one, then flirt
with some young creep who made sure to let me know he
was not talking to me. I would get stuck with the bill as
though I was still her agent trying to wine and dine her or
thank her for working with me. I actually couldn't afford to
go out with her right now.

"I set up a date on that app you downloaded for me during
our drunken night out last time." I looked down at my legs
and noticed I was wearing a very dumpy outfit and I knew
Julie probably looked like a model in her sweatpants, working from home. "I told some random guy I would meet him
in the Mission."

"Oh my god, what guy, the Indian? Or Israeli?"

"Indian, I think. But from California. He's all sorts of swag-
ger. Twenty-seven, according to his profile. Hopefully, he's
not younger than that and pretending to be older. Anyway,
Granny's got a young one."

"Stop that! You're not old."

"Easy for you to say, you're ten years younger than me!"

"Seriously, stop talking about yourself that way. You look
good for your age!" Julie was the queen of backhanded com-
pliments. She was a beautiful, impossibly thin, tall, brunette,
stylish woman lucky enough to inherit the best features from
both of her ancestral genetic pools. Whenever we went out
together, I had the feeling I was the ugly friend, and it often
seemed like men were trying to disable me to get to her. She
loved that attention too—really ate it up and wanted more.
It was very boring and annoying and slightly dangerous for
me sometimes.

"Oh my god, I can't just hook up with people like that."
Julie didn't have a problem expressing her opinions like I did.

"Yeah, I know, you told me that. Not everybody can be
so picky."

"I'm just a bitch."

"You're not a bitch. Don't say that."

"Yeah, no, I'm a bitch. Oh, I guess I'll go to the café to work. Well, have fun!"

"Unlikely."

She groaned and laughed at me with her throaty laugh. "Oh, I forgot to tell you. There's this guy in my building, he's older, but I think he's sort of handsome. I think you should go out with him…"

"How old?"

"I'm not sure, maybe fifty-eight?"

"Jeez, that's too old. Guys have a lot of baggage by that age."

"I don't know, I think he's kind of hot. You should go out with him! I'm going to give him your number."

"Nooooo, Julie!"

"Too late! Haha."

"Great. What's his name?"

"Nate. My neighbor thinks he's cranky. I would do him though!"

"I have a client calling. I have to go."

"Okay, call me later!"

I answered the incoming call. It was a young woman I had met two weeks ago at an open house and took to see a few properties during the following days. She had really liked one that happened to be intentionally underpriced and in one of the best areas.

"I talked to my dad and I'd like to make an offer at asking."

"Okay, well it's not going to sell for asking."

"Okay, but that's what I'm willing to offer."

"I totally get it, but this property is intentionally underpriced. It's going for at least two hundred thousand dollars over asking. I'm not trying to discourage you. But it's most likely not going to sell for asking."

"Look, that's fine if somebody wants to pay more for it, but this is the offer I am willing to make. We have cash, which I'm sure will make our offer appealing."

"Right, but they are going to have other cash offers." The place was a really desirable and rare property type, very much like a freestanding house but technically a condo, so a much better price point than a house.

"Are you saying I shouldn't bother? I mean, that's fine, we don't have to make an offer."

"No, of course not. I mean, you never know," I said, although I knew almost 100 percent that we didn't have a shot in hell. "I'll make any offer you want as long as you understand it's not likely to be accepted."

"That's fine. I'd also like the ability to cancel the offer for thirty days."

"What? Why?" Nobody would accept this terrible offer she was telling me to write.

"I won't find out if I have a job here for thirty days so I need the right to cancel the contract until I find out."

"Well, I can't tell them that! They will never accept an offer with that clause if I explain that to them."

"Isn't that what you get paid for? Negotiating? Making the deal?"

"Yes, and I'm telling you that you are not in a position to negotiate because there will be competition for this property. You have to make your best offer upfront. I'm just telling you that a contingency to back out for thirty days is not in any way competitive."

"I feel like you're trying to negotiate with me. Aren't you supposed to be on my side?"

"I am on your side, but I don't want to waste your time." *Or mine.*

"I'm not sure why this is so difficult. I've told you what offer I want to make. Why aren't you making the offer I want to make? Isn't that what you get paid for? To do what your client tells you to do?"

"Yes, like I said, I'll make any offer you want to make. That's not a problem. Although just to let you know, I only get paid if your offer actually gets accepted and you actually buy the place."

"Oh, sorry to hear that." She didn't sound sorry.

"Look, I'll write up the offer and send it to you to sign." *It's not going to get accepted at asking anyway.* "I'll put in a request that your dad be able to approve the property, and then if—"

By some act of God…

"—you get into contract, we'll just extend the contingency forever when your dad doesn't show up." This was going to be the absolute worst offer.

"Whatever you think is best." No way were we getting this property, and not because it was such a great place or because Tab is particularly good at marketing or selling anything. I groaned at the thought of having to talk to Tab but headed to his office anyway.

I found myself in the doorway staring at Katy.

"Hi," she said to me, looking up sheepishly, eyes wide and as surprised to see me there as I was to see her. I forgot she would be in that office. That meant she was fully on their team, maybe salaried. I glanced at the brochures by her side and saw that they now showed all three of them—Tab, his mom, and Katy—on all their marketing, fresh meat next to their bloated cadavers. I took her surprised expression to mean that she couldn't believe what she had been willing to do to get there. It seemed plausible that she had climbed her way up into the lap of one of the guys, either Tab's or Bryce's (he could have handed her off to Tab). It was sad to me that for all her climbing, she ended up in Tab's office, this fucking overgrown toddler who thinks himself a great real estate agent. As though being a real estate agent requires any intellect or talent whatsoever.

"I've got a buyer telling me she wants to make an offer at asking," I began, standing in the doorway.

"Offers are due today at twelve," she said, looking at me innocently. *Barely Legal,* I thought. She looked slightly uncomfortable like she didn't really want to be there.

"And I was just wondering, I didn't run any comps yet and I don't know if this buyer has what it takes, but I was wondering, are you expecting it to go over one point eight?" I asked her even though I doubted she would know.

"Yes, I think so," she said, without any attitude whatsoever.

I was slightly disarmed by her earnestness. Also, I had expected to hate her but instead, I felt bad for her.

"Okay, thanks. I just wanted to check, but that's what I thought." What I really wanted to ask her was: did she actually feel good about herself? What did she have to do to get on Tab's team? Had she gone to visit Bryce at his house, had he touched the small of her back, had he told her she looked sexy? Had she engineered her ascent into Tab's office, and was it all she'd dreamed of? Was she really trying to get somewhere big and did she think she had failed or was she just aiming low because her husband made most of the money and she was wearing that fat rock? I wanted to know, did she like Bryce? Did she cheat on her husband? Was she really slutty or did she just use her youth and sex as leverage, a bargaining chip? *It must turn her on because sex is power. I answered my own question.*

Chapter 8

Squandering Time at the Office

I T WAS MORNING, THE FIRES WERE STILL RAGING, and the smoke was spreading. Time moved sideways on those days when the sun was orange, and I didn't want to go outdoors. It was just waiting, waiting for it to be over. The power was still out in Marin, and that meant no cell service, no internet, and no way to make coffee.

A blanket of dirty air and ash mixed in with the dry heat made it very hard to breathe and go about life as usual. There was a moment when I realized that the ash and dust and little specks floating through the air were particles of incinerated beings, cremated remains of the unfortunate people who died in the fires. I was also breathing in the remnants of all the materials and belongings that had once adorned and composed peoples' homes: TVs and insulation, picture frames and drywall, paint and wallpaper, roofing, internet cables, plastic storage sheds, Barbies and Transformer figures, stuffed animals, Lego sets, bicycles, hamster wheels, refrigerators, toaster ovens, spare paint and paint remover, pictures and heirlooms, winter coats, camping gear, and hot tub covers, everything you can imagine that's toxic when burned and can kill you from just the fumes.

At night it was so spooky, not only because I was worried about how the fire might come to me, but because it felt like all the spirits of those who died were being released and the animal and human energies were lost, unable to find their way after being displaced, stopping by my bed on the way to wherever they were going after they had left their bodies.

"You can pass through but you can't stay," I would say when I felt one of them hesitating at my bedside, unsure if what I felt was real or if my sadness and fear had conjured it. Poor animals, I thought. Poor old people in their homes. Poor trees and plants. Poor families. Poor humans, this planet is toast and there's no safe place to live.

It was Wednesday, and there was an office meeting, even though the world was ending. Selling real estate in the city never has much concern about drought, social disintegration, or fires raging all over the state. Of course, there were always the agents who would send out periodic marketing about their efforts to build shacks for poor people in other countries, but mainly to get more business or (I suspected) to get laid.

I took the bus to work before sunrise so I wouldn't have to keep worrying about my car all day. I had recently discovered the luxury of Marin Transit busses, the quality of which surprisingly eclipsed the hostage situation simulation one encountered on SF's Muni Transit system. The bus was comfortable and air-conditioned, and one of the windows near my head was squeaking as it moved in its frame. There were large yellow releases at the bottom of each window. I couldn't tell exactly how they functioned by looking at them, but I knew I would figure it out if the bus flipped over and caught on fire. I am always prognosticating the worst-case scenario and planning for it since I'm an expert at surviving emergency situations. It was eerie to pass through the progression of still-dark cities with no working streetlights or stoplights, no power at gas stations, no open stores. I stared out the window as I rode, hoping nobody would sit next to me. Eventually, a judgmental-looking lady did, though she perched on the edge of the seat like she wanted to stay as far from me as possible.

My phone suddenly started buzzing with porn text messages. The lady saw it before I could obscure her view.

I shifted my body so she couldn't see the screen any longer,
but there was the problem of the guy behind me as well, who
could probably see through the space between the seats.
They kept arriving on my phone with an annoying buzz,
and I was compelled to look at each one: graphic images of
couples fucking in little action loops. I felt an internal flinch
with every new message. Every time I let my guard down or
thought I was in the clear, another picture arrived, jarring
me internally. I didn't respond. It was the young guy from
last night. I had told the kid not to send me porn because I
use my phone so much for work, but he was doing it anyway. I regretted the hookup. I had known from the moment
I matched with him that I would not find him attractive or
interesting or anything, but I proceeded almost compulsively.

I don't know if I have sex with strangers because I'm lonely
and incapable of regular relationships or because I'm a sex
addict. Sometimes I think I do it because it's what everybody
seems to be doing and sometimes I tell myself I'm empowered because I'm taking care of my needs, although the sex
is rarely satisfying and I feel a good amount of revulsion after.
I was getting near the office, and the texts were jangling my
nerves. I blocked him. Too much stress and now the office.

I joined the scrum of agents entering the elevator. The main
floor of the office was packed with folding chairs and more
agents. There was a projection of a slide onto the back wall:

♋

Welcome, Great Agents,
to the First meeting of June 2019!

♋

Some Food for thought:
Do you know who your clients are talking to?
Most people know 7 agents.

♋

How are you staying top of mind with clients?
Don't be a Secret Agent!
How are you going to make the most of Q3 2019?
Make a business plan now.

♋

Remember, 100% is easier than 90%.
Always be reaching out. 5 touches a day.
Let's make the most of the rest of the year.
Only six months left!

♋

I felt tired just looking at it. I headed to the standing area at the back of the rows of chairs, trying to be as invisible as possible so nobody could see my roots growing in, the damage to the heels of my shoes, or the pilling on my skirt.
I used to think it was cool to wear worn-out clothes but now I feel like I should throw them away after I've worn them two or three times.

"Let's get started!" A voice boomed above the agents as I walked into the office just in time for the meeting. I was immediately filled with dread upon hearing Tab's voice. He wasn't supposed to be leading the meeting this week.

"Let's get started! I have a really great, new, four-bedroom Victorian single-family, amazing remodel, Russian Hill. Chef's kitchen, all bedrooms on the same floor, views of the Golden Gate Bridge, a four-car garage, and you can park an additional two if you block the driveway. It's really a great property. Just exceptional if you've got a qualified buyer. We had the seller redo the kitchen and baths. It's staged and ready to go. Janie has seen it." He gestured in Janie's direction. "And she can concur; this is a top-tier property." Janie, a self-important, sixty-something agent with nice hair and a pear-shaped body and who always has huge listings nodded in response.

Tab continued. "It's tentatively six point nine, off-market for now while we assess demand. Let me know if you want to get your clients in before we go to market."

I was bored already. None of it was helpful to me or had anything to do with the business I do. Tab continued to boast about his giant, expensive listing, practically bursting at the seams with pride while his mother Brenda sat in the audience in front of him, her face warped and stretched like a melted, plastic clown doll. *She looks like a Weeble Wobble that got left on the cooktop.* I don't know why I hated them so much but I think I sensed they had an unfair advantage. I don't think the big agents in my office are aware of how obvious their advantage is, or perhaps they would tone down their pretentious bragging.

I submitted my terrible offer to Tab and Brenda via email at noon. Katy sent back an email saying it had been received and that they would be getting back to us in the afternoon. I parked myself at a vacant floater station and sent emails to prospects, otherwise squandering time.

Chapter 9

An Inappropriate Activity for an Agent Who Is Supposedly Working

I N THE LATE AFTERNOON, I HAD A SHOWING only a few blocks from our fancy office in a squalid area besieged by Central American drug dealers, local criminals, and drug customers—people living hard lives. The convenience store at the end of the block regularly had people robbing them in broad daylight, jumping over the counter to help themselves to the more expensive items. The employees had been instructed not to interfere, and the criminals had gotten the word: everything in the store is free and the DA wouldn't prosecute such crimes. The building with my low-end listing was in the middle of the block, and the two commercial spaces on either side of the lobby appealed to tech workers by accepting cryptocurrency, selling individual drip coffees made to order for $10 each, and allowing customers to wear pajamas and sit in the cafes and work for hours on end.

I was early and waited on a hard sofa in the ugly lobby of the building. The sofas flanked the entrance to a utility room, and the maintenance man said hello to me as he went in and out of his closet. The agent sent me a text to let me know she was running late. An hour late. *That's fine. It's not as though this job is that hard.* Meanwhile, the maintenance guy was friendly, and I was friendly in return. Once we exchanged pleasantries though, he just kept lingering.

"Would you like a coffee?"

"Sure, I will get a coffee with you."

"If I buy a giant pastry and only want a quarter, do you want the rest?"

"Yes, I will take anything you don't want."

We were in agreement. We went to the coffee shop by the entrance of the condo complex. He followed me through the café checkout, and we made small talk while we waited for our coffees.

"Where are you from?"

"I am from Guatemala."

"Oh, I see."

"Are you married?"

"No, not married."

"Kids?"

"I would never do that to a child," I joked, but he didn't get it.

"What you wouldn't do?"

"No, I was joking. Never mind."

"Oh. Oh, ha ha ha!" He let out an enthusiastic laugh.

Everybody in the café was probably twenty years younger than me and seemed to be communicating in a coded language. I imagined they had no idea what they were looking at while this tight-ass saleslady strolled socially with the short, balding, pot-bellied maintenance guy.

We got our coffees and our dissected pastry and we went back to the lobby and chatted.

"You are really not married?"

"Not married. I was doing the online thing but I'm not very good at it."

"Oh, really?" I felt his attention on me, and it made me feel embarrassed.

"Have you tried it?" I asked him.

"Oh, yes, I have tried it. Sometime." His English was a little choppy, but he was perfect at following the emotional arc of a story.

"Seems like everybody is doing it. I don't know how else to meet people. But the dates are awful."

"Oh, you had a bad date? How did it go? Tell me."

"I had a guy walk out on me!"

"No, really?" he gushed.

"I met this guy online and I knew immediately I didn't really like him, but he was so persistent, he just kept asking. He was handsome in his photo. So, I get to the bar, and he's not there yet, which is bad because I'm looking around, and it's embarrassing because I feel like everybody can tell I am looking for somebody I have never met. And I sit there alone, waiting, and the bartender is this sort of mean lady and she keeps asking if I want a drink. I repeatedly tell her that I am waiting for somebody and that they are coming, but she tells me I will have to move from the bar if I'm not going to order a drink."

"Oh, so you kept waiting…?" he added, trying to stay involved in the story.

"So, I order a drink, and finally the guy comes, my online date, and he looks sort of angry already. He sits next to me and orders his own drink. He starts telling me about his life, and I can tell we are probably not compatible for various lifestyle reasons—like he lives near his ex-wife and has shared custody of two teenage kids."

"Do you like kids?" He started wandering away from the storyline.

"Sure. So, I'm still willing to let the guy convince me that we should go dancing or something. Then he asks me if I want to have another drink, and I tell him no, I'm just having one drink because I don't want to drive drunk. And he just gets up and leaves! He walks out."

"Oh, what? He leaves you?"

"Yeah! He just gets up and leaves! No, 'I'm sorry,' no, 'excuse me,' nothing. Unbelievable. So rude!"

"Oh my gosh, I can't believe it." He was following along so well, and I felt validated by his shared outrage.

"Yeah, so rude!"

"I would never do that. I mean, I will take you dancing."

"Yeah. Crazy. Oh, dancing?"

"Yeah, I will take you dancing or a coffee."

"Like we just had coffee?" I asked him, slightly dismayed and alarmed.

"Yes, I don't know, or we could get a coffee." I was starting to wonder if we had a language problem or if it was an issue of comprehension.

"We just had coffee."

"I only need an hour."

"You only need an hour? For what?" He was starting to irritate me.

"Yes, I only need an hour and then you can see if you want more."

"Oh boy, I didn't know," I said with growing gloom.

"What?" he asked weakly.

"You're trying to seduce me," I said.

"I just, we could have coffee, I just need an hour." I rolled my eyes, still not taking him seriously. Then he blurted, "I will kiss you all over your body."

I shut my mouth and stopped talking, unable to come up with any additional harmless banter. It had not been my intention to flirt with the guy; I was just being nice. I laughed it off while a pit of dread opened up inside me. I looked at his face and saw he had nice lips, not too bad, but he had a funny nose, and his head was sweating so much that his thinning comb-over was looking wispy and spread out. I tried not to look at his face too closely. The best description of it after a once-over would be "funny-looking" or "squishy." I quit engaging with the guy and looked back down at my phone.

The agent finally showed up. The maintenance guy went away, and I did the showing. The agent had turned out to be nice if a bit ditzy, and the buyer seemed legitimate, if somewhat distracted. I escorted them back to the exit and said goodbye. They left, and the maintenance guy was back on my case, sticking to my side like a suckerfish.

"So that was the buyer?"

"Yes."

"And how did they like it?"

"I don't know yet." This guy was really irritating me now with his earnest inquiries about what had just transpired. It was boring when it actually happened in real life and it was not becoming less boring while recounting it.

"What are you doing now?"

"I'm leaving."

"Oh, do you want to get something to eat? I could go on break."

"No, I have to work."

"Oh, yeah, I have to work too. We can take a break together. For an hour?"

"No, I have to go to the office." I didn't want to be rude, but I needed to get rid of the guy. He followed me back up to the condo, talking more of his boring talk, stopping at the front door. I went in and stood in the hallway looking at him. He wasn't going to go away. Even if I closed the door in his face, he would probably be standing there when I came back out. And if not, he was going to be lurking in the hallway or the lobby. I felt obligated to manage his expectations because I gave him the wrong idea by being too open and too nice. Irritated, I gestured for him to come in.

"You want me to come in?"

"Okay, you can come in. Come in." I said bossily, with some resignation and impatience.

He waddled in, and I told him to take a seat. I guided him to the corner of the bed, which broke, comically. I straddled him on the corner of the drooping bed and started grinding on him. He ran his hands over my legs multiple times, then lifted my dress and palpated my breasts. I felt through his pants for his dick, like a doctor. I don't know what I would have done if it had been a giant, beautiful cock waiting for me in those blue workman's pants; what I found was more like a baby gherkin.

"You have a nice cock," I encouraged.

"You are so beeyoutiful," he said, shaking and grabbing for me all over, unsure of which body part to fondle first. I was enacting a porn plotline. He was delirious, excited, like he couldn't believe all his persistence had finally paid off.

Trembling, he sat on the edge of the bed and positioned me standing in front of him. He yanked my stockings and panties down and absolutely buried his face in my crotch, licking at me voraciously. There was so much slobber coming from his enormous mouth, and I tried not to watch. He grabbed at me, shaking as though he had palsy. I ran my hand through the damp, moist, thinning hair spread out in limp strands over his bumpy pumpkin head. He was not attractive. I looked up and saw myself in the mirror. I looked pretty good, I mean, I looked old and I used to be prettier, but not too bad, thinner than I usually look to myself. My hair needed to be dyed again but it was pulled up neatly in little twists and secured with bobby pins. I had this cute little black dress on and a crepe scarf with gold flecks around my neck. Over-the-knee boots. I don't wear them often but when I do, it seems like some guy tries to have sex with me. For sure it's those boots.

He worked on me relentlessly, his head buried between my legs, his saliva copious, his focus absolutely concentrated. It was sleazy, and he was so turned on and working with such enthusiasm that I orgasmed pretty quickly, thankfully, my eyes rolling back in my skull. I may have grabbed his head and suffocated his face but I'm not sure—I blacked out for a moment there. As soon as I had my orgasm, I felt immediately bored and I just wanted to get out of there. It was an ugly little condo. You don't get much for half a million dollars in San Francisco, just a view of City Hall and a farmer's market of illegal drugs if you want to walk half a block from your building to the convenience store.

I have never had sex at any of my listings, but for some reason, this seemed acceptable to me. Never again. Business unfinished, I dragged the handyman guy by the arm to the bathroom. I should have put the toilet seat up, but I didn't.

He kept trying to get me to turn around, I assumed to fuck me without protection, but I would not let him. I told him I would jerk him off, even though I already felt mostly revulsion for him. I wet my hand with tap water and stroked his uncircumcised cock, which seemed even smaller now and slightly sad looking. It looked gross. I stroked him for about twenty-three seconds, an eternity, and he told me he was coming. He shot his sperm on the toilet seat, the toilet bowl, and the floor. It was repulsive, but I was practical, like a doctor or crime scene cleaner. I wiped up the semen with toilet paper and he helped me. I didn't notice until later the stains on my dress.

We went back down the elevator, and he exited at the lobby level where some vendor was waiting for him. I peeked out so that I could be seen, in case he wanted to brag about it to a friend later. I watched this odd-looking, short man with stringy, wet hair walk toward them with their expectant faces. *Maybe they feel sorry for him,* I thought. I should feel sorry for myself. I have casual sex with people I am not even attracted to. I pretend that I'm liberated but I don't even know what I want and if I did, I doubt I could advocate for myself to get it. I headed to the mezzanine level where there was a second exit so I could do my daytime walk of shame without witnesses. It had started to rain. I received a text message from my new maintenance man friend, then another, then another. I blocked him.

MORE THAN SIX HOURS HAD PASSED SINCE I HAD SUBMITTED that offer for my loser client, even though Tab and Katy assured us that they would be getting right back to us since they had demanded the strict offer date and time. Finally, finally, night having fallen, the whole day having been spent waiting, Tab the overgrown toddler called me.

"This is Ruby."

"Hi, may I speak to Ruby please?"

"Yes, this is Ruby. This is Ruby." I repeated myself so that
I didn't have to hear Tab ask for me again after I had already
announced my name once and confirmed it a second time.

"Yes, I'm calling about your offer on…"

"Yes, the offer we submitted today at twelve noon, your
deadline."

"Yes. Yours was the lowest. Not a very strong offer…it's a
shame to waste everybody's time like that."

"Yeah, well, she's young. She's nervous." I didn't know
why I was defending her. I should have been berating him for
not cutting us loose earlier.

"I was twenty-three when I bought my first property. Being
young is no excuse."

"Right. Better luck next time."

"It's about more than luck."

"Yeah, that's just a saying." My hatred was festering.

"If you want my advice, you should find some better clients
to represent." He hung up. *How fucking helpful.*

It was ineffectual San Francisco rain: wispy and whiny, not
a real rain like they have on the south or the east coast. I still
had a good twenty minutes of walking to catch the night
bus, then forty minutes riding, then another ten walking to
get home. First, I needed to drop off the keys to my listing
for another agent to pick up from the office. The building
was dark—too late for most agents to be working. I stepped
in some shit by the entrance and had to spend five minutes
scraping my shoe on the curb. I was pretty sure it was human
shit. I gave up eventually, figuring it would get absorbed into
the office carpet.

I had headed into the building's lobby and called for the
elevator when a woman came to the door and entered the
lobby after me. I glanced sideways and saw stiletto ankle
boots and tight black leggings, inappropriate real estate agent
attire. It was Katy. She was wearing totally different clothes
than she had been wearing earlier today like she was going
on a date. She had stubby fingernails with dark polish and
still that giant rock and wedding ring. Her bright, young,

made-up face was framed by her curled hair on which she had obviously exerted a ton of effort.

"Hi," I told her once we were in the elevator together.

She smiled at me brightly. "I'm about ready for this rain to stop," she said. I had no response, partly because I was sleep deprived. But also, I just didn't have a response.

"Oh, yeah?" I couldn't come up with anything better. There was just no room in my brain with so many thoughts running through it about everybody and everything. She was then equally stumped as to what to say. She sauntered off, her tiny butt bouncing and flapping down the hall as she walked. *Somebody has definitely been banging her.*

Chapter 10

When You Let Yourself Get Taken

FRIDAY, I WAS SET TO MEET JULIE AT RANDY'S, a neighbor-hood bar in the Marina, mainly because I wanted to tell her all about my horrible date the night before. Julie was the one who had encouraged me to get right back on the gross online dating app thing, even though I had told her that I thought I was a danger to myself. I couldn't wait to horrify her with all the details. I was on time, sat myself at the bar, and waited for her for twenty minutes. I tried to nurse my glass of house wine because I had to drive back to Marin. Julie was taking a cab.

"Hey girl," Julie said musically as she stood at the entrance and pushed her long hair off her shoulder, immediately draw-ing the attention of every man in the bar. Everywhere we went, the same thing happened—all the dumb dudes would see her and then get this far-away look on their faces as though they were the only guy to ever spot such a treasure, as though they had found the answer to what had been miss-ing in their lives, what would make them complete, what would prove they were special and smart and successful and had arrived and whatever else they were looking to prove. It was always young dudes with a chip on their shoulder who were attracted to Mistress Impossible, this beautiful specimen of a woman.

Julie looked stunning, as usual, with her stylish trench over wide-leg seventies-style pants and a very low-cut silk blouse, plus large statement earrings. She was flat-chested, but it didn't matter because she had long legs, a great ass, perfect hair, full lips, and a very pretty face, although her nose was really too small in relation to her other features. She knew how to act very nice too, but it was a put-on. "I'm a bitch," is what she always told me, and although I tried to convince her otherwise, it was actually true. She was proud of it, and the guys who liked her were turned on by it.

She came over to the bar and hugged me in a performative way. She was wearing a tasteful amount of perfume, but I felt like it was covering up the smell of farts or something slightly rotten. She denied having an eating disorder, but I had seen the tiny rations of food she would eat at home, five little cubes of sweet potato at a time, and I knew she was probably forcing herself to vomit after every meal. She not only denied it but she also always made an effort to eat a full meal in front of me to prove how much she ate. She would tell me that I had body dysmorphia any time I said I wanted to lose weight, even though I was most certainly twenty pounds too heavy for my height and frame.

Julie sat on the stool next to me, picked up the menu, and looked around the bar, then groaned. "Ugh, it looks like all tech dudes in here." She let out a little burp while reaching for a wine list.

"Yeah, I think one of them brought a Segway."

"Gross." She waited until the bartender was in front of us and then asked to taste three different wines.

"Here's the happy hour menu." I pushed it toward her, and she gave it a cursory look. She asked to taste the three most expensive wines while I sipped my house wine.

"I'm starving." She pushed the happy hour menu away and grabbed the full menu. "Will you eat some if I get the steak?"

"Oh, I ate before I came here. I'm not really hungry."

"One steak. Oh, and the crab cakes. And the lobster appetizer, please." She handed the menu to the bartender and

began to taste the wines he had poured for her. I sighed.
I wasn't hungry, and she had just ordered what had to be all
the most expensive items on the menu.

"I'm really not hungry at all," I told her, but she just
shrugged. When the food arrived, she helped herself and
asked for a small plate, then proceeded to dump half of
each dish onto the smaller plate.

"Eat. Have some," she dictated as though she were taking care of me. She had the bartender bring utensils for me
and eventually, of course, I had some of it, even though
I was on a budget and had eaten before we got there to save
money. I was shorter and fatter than Julie, so I really didn't
want to be her garbage disposal or weight control device.
Every time we went out, it was the same thing: she ordered
a sumptuous array of dishes, forced me to eat half, chopped
everything into weird little pieces, then headed to the bathroom after eating. The bartender flirted with her, and she
greedily soaked up the attention. She ordered another drink
for me.

"I have to drive home. I don't want to drive drunk."

"Here." She pushed a water toward me as if drinking
water would keep me from blacking out on my way home.
Last time I had woken up to find myself on some winding
road in Tiburon trying to program my GPS while driving.
Very bad. Tiburon isn't even on my way home.

"So, what happened last night?"

"I've been dying to tell you about it."

"Was he hot?"

"What? No! He was that weird guy in that red sweatsuit that
looked like sports pajamas."

She and the bartender looked at each other with sexy eyes,
and he came by and filled Julie's glass with water. He ignored
mine.

"Oh my god, that guy? What about my neighbor? Did you
talk to him? Are you going out with him Saturday?"

"I don't know, he's so old! I'm trying to tell you about last
night."

But Julie was checking her phone, then the menu, then
talking to the bartender. I wanted to talk to her about
how I wasn't sure whether my sexual activities evidenced
empowered desire or addiction. But Julie never cared about
self-examination and she had a short attention span for the
struggles of anybody other than herself, so I was on my own
with recovering from the experience. I had picked that guy
almost randomly last night, a blurry-faced guy wearing what
looked like pajamas or sportswear. The wine was kicking in,
and without any actual human interaction, I began to lose
myself in the memory, partly reciting it in my mind so that it
would be fresh for retelling.

The guy had been holding a flag and he was with a crowd
of other guys. At a soccer match? In Gaza? I didn't care. I sent
him a message.

You are handsome, I lied while looking at the ugly outfit.
He certainly didn't appear to be hot in any way. He looked
like a rodeo clown.

Where do you live?

I live in Marin but I can come to you.

We met at a cheap bar in Oakland, and I confirmed when
I saw him that I was not attracted to him. I felt dead. I felt like
cardboard, flat. In person, he appeared to be wearing the
same outfit he was wearing in his online photo—some cheap,
red sweatshirt thing and matching leisurewear pants that
looked like they could accommodate a diaper. He asked me
if I wanted to come over. I stammered for a while in response
while enormous judgments lumbered around in my mind.
No, I don't want to come over.

"Okay," I said. "I'll follow you."

"We can take my car. There's no street parking, and
I don't have any guest spaces, so we need to take one car.
It's in the hills. I'll drive." I went with him while my eyes
forlornly stayed on my car. As we drove, he pointed out
a house on a hill. "That place has very nice views. I have
been inside that one. The owners are never home." He had
a foreign accent.

58

"Oh, okay," I said. Was he telling me so that I understood that there was nobody to hear me scream? I was so stupid to agree to take one car. That meant he would have to drive me back to my car after whatever happened, which meant I had better behave and agree to whatever he wanted, like a Taliban prisoner. He probably thought he was being a gentleman. I checked my phone and there was no coverage.

We got to his place, and so far, so good: I was still alive. I gingerly followed him into the house, and we stood in the hideous kitchen for a bit, a garish remodel. The kitchen smelled of old oil, and the scent of rotting food wafted up periodically from the sink drain. We tried to have a conversation but didn't find that we had anything in common. I couldn't even understand what he was saying because his accent was getting stronger.

The house was on a hill, and the bedrooms were downstairs, the walls of which were a hideous dark blue color. I sat on the bed and just started taking my clothes off. He stood there in his clown pants, watching me while he stood to the side of his giant, king-plus-size bed. It appeared to be the size of two queens put together. I started to disassociate. I came back to the room as he was shoving my head toward his dick. I resisted but I also submitted. *I hate this guy.* It was a rude thing to do to a stranger. There was clearly no pretense of chivalry now, not that I believed there was before. I did it even though I hated his guts and I knew he didn't care how I felt about him or what I thought about him.

His attitude and behavior remind me of the boys in high school: focused on getting what they wanted, always on the hunt, coercing us, colluding and rating us, isolating and tricking us into compromised positions. It was a long list too, stretching back over time with boys I knew, boys I didn't know, grown men, strangers on the streets or in the hallways or driving in cars, employers, TV, and the media, and also the women who internalized their attitudes and reinforced the hierarchy, or I guess it was the patriarchy. And I always just went with it and maybe I assumed I was to blame or it was all normal, or at least that I could handle it, or that I had wanted it, or even now that I was the one in control of it. And I told myself it didn't impact me but I didn't know that these things add up over time until you are under a giant weight, suffocating or gasping for air because it's all you can do to keep your head above water.

I let my teeth periodically graze his dick as though I were terrible at giving him head. He said nothing but he tried to readjust his dick so that it would slide to the back of my throat without hitting my teeth. Every time he readjusted, I gagged a little and went right back to grazing his dick with my teeth so that he would stop trying to fuck my mouth. *Fuck this guy. I'm so fucking bored by this annoying person.*

I eventually shoved his hand off my head and started giving him a hand job because I was already tired of keeping my jaw wrenched open and I fucking hated the guy. I jerked him off for a while, but he wasn't having an orgasm. *Probably because he watches porn all the time in his huge gross bed and his dick is numb.* I mentally checked out again and when I came back, I was getting dressed. I had only consumed one glass of wine.

Hours later, I was home. It occurred to me that I was very lucky I hadn't picked a guy who wanted to strangle me and cut me up into pieces. I had been lucky so many times, not really lucky, but lucky it hadn't been worse. I blamed myself for going with him, for all of it, for choosing him and bringing myself to him like a free prostitute, but I still hated the guy. I wanted to punch him in the head, I hated him that much. And then I felt shame for not being able to have normal relationships and for putting myself in such a disempowering situation. *Why do I continue to behave this way? It has to be an addiction, but to what? And what caused it? And why can't I stop it since I know I am doing it?*

I had started down the flashback vortex, probably triggered by Julie ignoring me. I think she might have sensed it because she glanced at me quickly, then took the phone from me and navigated to the conversation. She picked

at her teeth while scrolling and reading. I don't think she
noticed that my eyes had started welling up with tears, my
breathing shallow. I was on the edge of tipping over into
my self-absorbed sorrow, but her lack of sensitivity helped
steady me a little. If I had been with somebody caring who
noticed and said something kind to me, it would have been
too much. I would have felt so sorry for myself as I imagined their empathy for me, and it would have consumed
me, the pity and sadness and bottomless angst for the poor,
empty creature, me. But Julie didn't care too much about
other people.

"Oh my god."

"Yeah."

"Was he hot at all?"

"Not in any way."

"Where did you go?"

"Some crappy bar in Oakland."

"Did he at least buy you dinner?"

"Why would I want to eat dinner with an ugly guy I don't
know?"

"God, I don't know, so that you get something out of it?
There are some amazing restaurants in Oakland! Look at that
guy's shoes—he has money! I would have told him we had
to go shopping on our date." She laughed a throaty laugh.

"He bought me a crappy glass of red wine."

"Oh."

Some guy next to Julie turned to her. "Can you pass me
that menu?"

"Sure."

I had been just about to launch into my story about the
previous night, but some turd had found a way to approach
Julie, so now I had to jockey for attention.

"How's your evening so far?" He was some skinny, young
dude with curly dark hair. He seemed like he was trying to
act suave but he just looked like another scrawny wannabe,
too middle of the road. Julie liked them to be beefier, manlier,
and way meaner or way nicer. She would crush this guy.

Julie was a trauma survivor as well from a broken home with a mentally ill, abusive mother and an alcoholic, neglectful father. Her parents divorced early on, and Julie fell into running with tough crowds. I felt sorry for her because she struggled with relationships and with functioning in the world, though her method of surviving seemed to be more parasitic than mine. She was usually trying to get whatever she could from any given situation or person. It was entertaining as long as it was directed away from me.

"Can't complain. How are you doing?"

"I read about this place online and wanted to give it a try." Such a boring dude. Like Julie hasn't heard a thousand similar opening conversations. "Do you live here?"

"Born and raised." She sat up straighter on her barstool and picked up her wineglass so that the cursive tattoo on her forearm was visible. She looked classy with an edge, though her tattoo was misspelled. This dude would never notice.

"And what do you do?" he asked Julie, gazing at her intently. I leaned forward in case I would have an opportunity to participate in the conversation, but he tried to block my view of him by sitting back so that Julie's head was in the way.

"I'm a real estate agent." He ignored me. Julie didn't make any attempt to include me either, as usual.

"I do cancer research," Julie said.

"Wow," he said, immediately falling in love with her.

Julie always used that line. She didn't actually do cancer research. She compiled data from cancer research that somebody else did. She basically did data entry. He scowled at me like I was getting between him and the vessel for his future progeny. Little did he know that Julie hated children and was no breeder. Worse than that, she did not like giving head and also was not capable of orgasm without at least an hour of direct stimulation from her partner. What she was capable of was letting a dude take her to expensive dinners, buy her nice coats and designer booties, or pay for her rent and health insurance for an indeterminate period of time.

I slumped over the bar, bored and disappointed that Julie was prioritizing attention from a guy I knew she would never go for. Maybe she derived some pleasure from the ritual of stringing a guy along and then stomping on his hopes.

Julie turned to me. "Is this asshole going to buy us a drink or what?"

The guy looked at her with worry. "So, should I get your number? Or should we connect on Facebook?"

Julie cut him off without mercy. "Oh, I don't think my boyfriend would like that."

"I can connect with you on Facebook," I offered, though I hate Facebook and am never on the site. He ignored me and packed up. Julie had ruined another guy. The bartender put our bill in a glass in front of us.

"Your treat! I paid last time," Julie announced and started putting her jacket on.

"You did? I don't remember that. Why did you order the most expensive wine?"

"Oh, did I? I just like good wine. I'm sorry." She gave me the fake frown face and kept getting ready to go, tossing her hair off her shoulders and checking her phone. I felt slightly drunk and I was worried about driving home. I put my credit card out for the bartender to run. I felt like I was Julie's boyfriend.

"Bye-eee," Julie cooed while looking at her phone and running to the door. Her ride had arrived. I took a sip from her water. The bartender hadn't refilled mine.

Chapter 11

A Date with the Neighbor Julie Mentioned

I CALLED JULIE'S NEIGHBOR, NATE. It was early Saturday evening when we met outside his condo in the dingy and dangerous—but trendy—Tenderloin. He was acting sort of shy, his hand in his droopy pants pocket, one foot balanced on the other.

"I don't think you remember but I met you at Julie's party last year. I guess you could say I've been waiting to go out with you for six months."

"I don't think that's true, but it sounds good." I was immediately infatuated but determined not to show it. He then surprised me by stepping forward and kissing me hello, a wholesome kiss with his big, lush lips. He was wearing an unusual outfit: sort of like an Italian, working-class dandy, boyish in his rolled-up jeans, newsboy cap, and striped, nautical-themed shirt, arm muscles bulging slightly. He looked younger than fifty-eight; Julie must have been wrong about that. He had on casual leather boots and a leather belt with an artisan, one-of-a-kind, retro buckle with an owl on it. His face was handsome. I thought he was very good-looking, but didn't act as if he thought so. He acted like he was modest. His hands were a little rough. His skin was tanned and dark, and he was manlier than most of the men I had dated. He was artistic, eccentric, different. He was introverted, shy, irritable, and maybe depressed.

It was early evening, not yet dark, and we walked at a moderate pace down the dirty street. The wind picked up, and something gritty blew into my eye. I checked my phone to see the location of the bar I was looking for, and he scolded me.

"Don't take your phone out around here! You're going to get jumped."

I looked at him like he was crazy but I could see that he was very serious. There were plenty of young, stylish people around us, probably going to their overpriced apartments or the overpriced concept bars, but they were intermingled with the original occupants of the neighborhood: stragglers who couldn't walk straight, angry-looking guys who didn't smell very good, presumed drug dealers and users, and crazy-looking ladies here and there who watched the urine-soaked sidewalk as they wobbled, looking for discarded cigarette butts to smoke. Amidst all this squalor, we made it to our destination, Europa, a concept bar on Geary Street. The ambiance was very dark, and the furniture was all sleek leather and wood, the pieces carefully curated, the rooms accented with Moroccan-style metal chandeliers.

We sat down right away on the stools in the middle of the bar, and Nate ordered an expensive bourbon drink while I ordered the least expensive drink I could find on the menu, a sparkling rosé. The bartenders were younger than us and only a little bit friendly or attentive. They were wearing all black and had the requisite forearm tattoos and facial hair or cleavage, depending on their gender. They were operating in their own world with their own physical language as they moved gracefully around inside the bar's enclosure, like fish in an aquarium.

We didn't finish our appetizer because it was too compli-cated—it involved steak tartare and some oil in a spoon plus crunchy fried-fat things for garnish and required some assembly. We joked a little and chatted.

"This place is fricking expensive. I could make this drink at home for free."

"How are you supposed to eat this thing?" I wondered.

"I've never thought of coming to a place like this."

"Oh—do you normally stick to dive bars?"

"Yes."

"Oh. Well, I didn't mean to force you to go to a fancy place."

"That's okay, I like fancy. I'm very able to be fancy."

"Yes, I can see that," I said, smiling as he held the tiny spoon that arrived with the complex appetizer, his pinky sticking out. "I'm glad you were willing to come here. I've been wanting to check it out. It was opened by this woman who was on one of those cooking competition shows."

"I like that you picked this fancy place with the expensive drinks. I love these large ice cubes. I'm getting some special ice cube trays so I can have big ice cubes for my drinks in my apartment. You should see my duck glasses. I got them at the flea market." It was the most effusive he had been all night, but he was not exactly gushing, more like ridiculing himself.

I was having a good time and I thought he was too but I wasn't sure. Normally after one big drink, I received some signal from the guy, like maybe he touched my arm or my hand or my leg. Then I would know that he was attracted to me or at least that he felt comfortable with me. But Nate had been keeping his body completely separate from mine. I couldn't even feel any heat coming from his body, that was how far he was sitting from me.

The kiss from earlier persisted in my memory, but the excitement I felt from it was starting to fade, like a stencil in the sand. If he were attracted to me, it would be normal at this point for him to touch me accidentally or intentionally to signal some interest, but there was nothing. It was so strange! I didn't think it was politeness or chivalry. It was just a big question mark hanging over the encounter. *Did I do something wrong? Is he not that interested in me?* I wondered if he was already seeing somebody. *Maybe he is seeing a number of women. Maybe he's in high demand.*

I paid for the first round, even though I felt I shouldn't. He didn't try to pay. He didn't even pretend to try to pay. I had invited him, so I acted like everything was cool and I didn't expect that anyway. I'm not a hustler and I'm not a gold-digger at all but I also would not be insulted if the guy had insisted on paying.

I was tipsy when we left, and as we walked, I wasn't sure if we were on a date or pretending to just be friends. He was exciting to me and funny, and I liked how he was spontaneous and willing to try anything. I thanked Julie in my mind for insisting that I make the date with him. He was adventurous and comfortable in this urban environment. He seemed to like the squalor in his neighborhood, preferring it to the gentrification, in fact, he mentioned "techie fuckers" at least twice while we were walking. I don't like the changes to the city either but I'm not angry at the random young people outnumbering us these days in every neighborhood. Of course, I don't like how they all wear their pajamas to cafes and stare at their laptops and recoil in horror if you start a conversation with any of them. It's a slow death of the San Francisco café culture, *but it was only ever delusional freaks I met at those cafés anyway, so I don't see it as that much of a loss.*

We arrived at another place a few blocks away, a deserted concept bar with mostly empty space. I guessed it would fill up later with throngs of drunken young people trying to talk over the loud music. It was more like a barn than a bar. We sat on stools in the front window like two old men and watched people on the street walk by. He went to the bar and came back with some cheap wine in a dirty glass. He paid for me this time.

We sat side by side, saying nothing, until he suddenly exclaimed, "I love this song!"

It was an awkward outburst. We fumbled forward through the rest of our time at the bar as we continued to watch the people walking by the front of our window. It was a strange date, getting stranger. He still hadn't touched me at all. I thought we were having a good time but I couldn't exactly tell whether he liked me in particular or if he was just lonely and needed somebody to hang out with.

We headed over to a third place, the Clift, the trendy hotel with the giant chair in the entry, taking turns sitting on it for fun, like characters in a 1980s music video. We checked out the bar area with the moving video portraits on the walls and we rode the elevators to see if there was anything exciting we could get into before we headed back to a seating area next to the grand lobby area. There were little light boxes on the walls illuminating drawings of animals: pigs, beavers, sheep. The whole place was so cute. I was tipsy. I wanted to touch him so badly that I took his hand in my hand. Why wasn't he touching me?

As I touched his hand, I asked him, "Nate, is this okay?"

"Yes, that's okay." He seemed pleased, but I also detected something like sarcasm. I don't know why everything he said seemed to be like he was making fun of me. It was subtle, so I just ignored it.

I touched his hand with mine, and we were quiet. I felt strongly attracted to him, crawling with sensual desire. I'm not sure why I was coming on to him. I never do that! I ran the back of my hand over his, caressing him, taking his fin-gers in my hand. We interlaced our fingers and let our hands sit there, warm and a little moist. We both looked ahead, toward and beyond our hands. We didn't have much to say, but it seemed fine to be quiet. Young women wearing too few clothes were gathering outside, lining up inside a velvet rope, anticipation building, waiting to be admitted to the nightclub in the hotel. The energy of the evening was starting to ramp up as the people visiting the neighborhood to party began to turn up their conversational volume. This hotel would have a long line around the block in a couple of hours, as the bar was fashionable and expensive, a real meat market. I wanted to get away from there. I preferred not to be a part of a rowdy party scene; also, I'm old. This was all the "going out" I really needed.

"Did you want to…"

"Yes," I said immediately.

"…maybe come over…"

"Yes," I deadpanned, trying to be blunt but funny.

"…and I could show you my duck glasses…"

I got up, taking his hand in mine, leading him out of there, knowing I wanted to get next to him, beside him, inside him, under his clothes, into his mind, anything. Something about him was driving me crazy.

We went back to his place, and I immediately took off my skirt and got on his couch. In my mind, I did so because I didn't want my skirt to get crumpled—it was pragmatic. I made myself comfortable on his sofa, pulling his fake-fur blanket over me while surveying the room. His place was very nicely decorated and it reminded me a bit of my grandmother. She had elegant taste and when she was alive, she wore Hollywood-style, fancy, high-heeled shoes and loved to smoke cigarettes.

He quickly joined me and we snuggled under the blanket. I felt so comfortable with him like we were just being cozy together on the couch. I didn't feel the usual pressure to put out or perform for him like a circus animal or let him bang me violently and pretend to be enjoying myself before having any opportunity to get turned on. He was so laid back that it almost compelled me to attack him. I am never that forward, that aggressive, though I was also sure to be cautious and gentle, like trying not to scare a deer away. Laying together, I touched him, and it was good, very sensual, with a lot of nuzzling. I kissed him softly and petted him tenderly. When I kissed him, it was not a bunch of tongue but more like coercing, eliciting a response, just like it had been all night on our date.

He was reserved and aloof in a way that was driving me nuts. I started grinding against his body, and he was seemingly responding, but it was more my effort than his. His dick was getting a little bit hard, but not rock hard, not raging. I figured he was a couple of years older than me and handsome like a mature French or Italian model, with his dark skin, brown eyes, and strong arms. He touched me gently, kissed my lips and neck, and caressed my head through my hair. After a while, and after confirming that his dick was hard enough that he was probably interested in having sex with me, I suggested that we go to the bedroom.

We climbed onto his bed where we got naked and began to have sex using a condom. He seemed very casual and experienced about the whole thing. Soon, he was on top of me, and it wasn't long before I told him that I could come at any time. He responded immediately and started thrusting into me, making me come, making us come together. I was impressed by how he knew to move his body with mine. When I told him I was coming, he responded and made it happen, unlike some guys who would instead stop what they were doing at a moment like that and do the opposite of what they had been doing, ruining everything. I hate it when guys do that. I shouldn't have to give a lecture or tutorial before a sexual encounter, but with some guys, that's what has to happen. I think they're trying not to come once I tell them that I am close, so they stop doing the exact thing that was going to make me come. Anyway, with Nate, it was really good, especially for the first time.

Afterward, he curled up with me and kissed the palm of my hand, so charming and romantic. He looked into my eyes for so long with his big brown eyes. He seemed vulnerable, and it was so charming to me. He caressed my hand with his thumb. I loved his meaty hands, like baseball mitts. He kissed me while holding my hands, a wholesome kiss, then looked into my eyes again. I looked at his thick brown hair in front of his eyes, his beautiful-looking chest—perfect. I felt so happy. Giddy.

He went to the bathroom and on the way, he asked, "Do you need a shirt to sleep in?"

"Sure," I said, surprised by the invitation. I was sitting up, naked, on the bed as he came back toward me. He tossed me a soft and worn shirt that mostly covered me. *He's lending me his clothes already,* I thought, and it made me feel so cozy.

I couldn't sleep. I was worried I might accidentally fart or snore and ruin his magical impression of me. I tossed and turned all night, feeling gross because I hadn't washed my face or brushed my teeth. I could feel a pimple growing next to my lip and I worried that maybe I had caught something from him or somebody else and wondered whether it would explode overnight and show him how unattractive and damaged I was in the morning.

When I woke up, he made me a coffee, kissed me, and seemed very happy I was there with him. He was so casual about it all and seemed so comfortable with my having stayed the night and being there in the morning. It felt almost like we were family. He walked me to my Mercedes and kissed me goodbye. As I drove away, I felt a night-after buzz, made heady by the lack of sleep. I stopped at a light a block from his place and casually watched a scene unfold from the comfort of my car. A raggedy-looking young woman was sitting on one of the benches built into the bus stop. In front of her was a Golden Retriever, its rear legs spread, bent, and trembling. A copious stream of diarrhea spewed from the dog's rear and formed a soggy mound in front of the bus stop, just before the curb. The owner remained seemingly unconcerned on her bench (she actually looked angry and indignant) while the dog relieved itself. She made no move to collect its shit, which I suppose would have been difficult since it was almost liquid. I doubt she was carrying any doggy poop bags, though. She looked like she lived and worked at that bus stop. Behind the bus stop, a man was lying on his side facing a building, his clothes discolored by variations of crusty substances. Up the hill from him, a bedraggled lady with a fallen face and missing teeth sauntered between the back of the bus stop and the horizontal man. As she pranced and swayed down the steep street, she yelled at nobody in particular, adamant about something. *This place is like Night of The Living Dead.* Then my light turned green, and I headed back to Marin, ignoring the squalor, taking it in stride. I was in love already. I was high.

Chapter 12
So in Love

IT WAS SUNDAY, AND I WAS SCHEDULED TO HOLD the open
house for Ugly-Jacket Lady. I wished I could have
stayed with Nate, maybe climbed onto the back of his
scooter and gone somewhere for brunch but unfortunately,
I am a real estate agent and I work on weekends. I felt like
I was going through withdrawal. I was still high from our
encounter, and I couldn't focus on anything, not that selling real estate requires more thought or consciousness than
it takes to drool. I was consumed by my thoughts of him.
We had not made any plans to see each other again.

"I had a really nice time," I told him in the morning before
he kissed me goodbye and sent me on my way, silently
turning and heading back to his condo. I had told him earlier that the sex was really good too. I wanted to be sure that
he knew how I felt, but he wasn't equally forthcoming.

The property was located half a small block from the
city jail, and just beyond the jail was the junky playground
of San Francisco—what I call the area of subsidized drug
use where the staggeringly inebriated mingled with the
Swiss-cheese-brained meth addicts in a fast-paced market
of squalor, also known as Skid Row. There's no effective
social help for the residents—they are just strung along
by the non-profits as well as strung out. If you dropped

anything of value in the gutter for even a second, it would be gone.

Because the loft's location was next to the jail, there weren't even any casual looky-loos coming by. The area contained a few lofts built in the 1990s but almost no retail or restaurants. Most of the parking spaces were reserved for official vehicles, so even if there were a restaurant, good luck getting to it. It was also one of those food deserts where there's no nearby grocery store only worse; this place didn't even have a corner store to sell you junk food.

On the weekdays it was legal offices and young lawyers in cheap suits, beefy cops, meter maids, 24-hour bail bondsmen, perps and their unfortunate families, of course, and maybe a taco truck in a small parking lot. On the weekend, the area cleared out—nobody lived there really; though today, there was a homeless guy sleeping in a doorway halfway down the alley. On weekends you were more likely to pass a homeless guy swaddled in dirty blankets staggering down the sidewalk than any other resident or tourist in the area. The zoning in the immediate area was mixed-use, so there were lots of small warehouses and then the "edgy" residential units mixed in. That's what my open house was, "edgy," though actually, it was completely pedestrian and bland. In any case, the area was dead. The air was still hazy and dry and burned my eyes as I put my heavy A-frame signs out.

Once inside, I began ruminating and fantasizing about Nate again, annoying myself, remembering the sex, the way he caressed me before we went to his bed, the way he kissed my hand after. It had been so hot, so good, so natural, and I wanted more, hours of it. We were so good together, and that had just been our first time. I replayed the images in my brain over and over, seeking more dopamine by conjuring the previous night, thinking about it so hard that I was overcome with lust and desire and had to lie down on the sofa. I was driving myself insane. Like a junky,

I needed to know that I would be getting more, but Nate wasn't making it clear that he was going to provide the supply. I waited to hear from Nate, but he didn't contact me.

Why won't he contact me when it was so good with us together? Am I being impatient? How quickly is time passing? Probably he has something interesting to do, and time isn't crawling for him the way it is for me at this mind-killing open house. Probably he is waiting to see how crazy I am, I warned myself but I couldn't help it; my crazy was coming out at the seams. I sent him another text saying that I had a great time and that I for sure wanted to see him again, even though I was repeating myself. I didn't care if he thought I was desperately ardent. I wanted him to know. I stared at my phone, waiting for a response that did not arrive. My skin was crawling.

The night before, he told me that he had been to Burning Man ten times. I didn't reply when he said it because I mostly try to act polite, but my thought was that it was weird that he told me that. I have no interest in Burning Man at all, so we were not compatible on this point, and I judge as odd most people who go to the event. To me, that was him telling me that there was something really wrong with *him,* but I didn't think about how it was simply a matter of us not being right for each other. I looked at it as a character flaw that I could maybe influence or ignore. I called my friend Julie and told her about the whole thing.

"Do you think he gave you drugs?"

"I don't know, I just, I mean, I feel so crazy. Oh, and he goes to Burning Man."

"Gross!"

"Every year."

"Disgusting. Oh my god. I hate Burning Man."

"Ten years in a row."

"Ugggh," she groaned. "Don't text him."

"It's too late."

"Oh my god. You have to stop."

"I had to let him know how I feel."

"You slept with him on the first date?" She was talking so quickly.

"Yes, well, he was really sexy but he was so aloof, I don't know, I couldn't tell if he liked me, and something about that just made me crazy. It's embarrassing. I feel out of control."

"Wow." Now she sounded like she was chewing on something.

"It was good."

"Ruby! You have to make him wait two days. Don't text him." She was definitely eating. I heard smacking noises.

"I feel crazy."

"Mmm. You have to be cool."

"I'm going crazy."

"You need to put your phone away and you need to not contact him for two days. Seriously."

"But I want him to know how I feel. I don't want to play games."

"Oh my god! You need to stop! Don't text him! Ruby, he's going to think you are crazy! Seriously, stop."

But I wouldn't stop myself.

There was no answer from him after fifteen minutes, and that seemed like forever to me considering he is somebody who is always looking at his phone when we are together. I didn't wait very long before I sent the next text.

I really want to have sex with you again. I hope that's okay that I said that.

Another five minutes and thirty-two seconds went by before he replied.

Totally fine!

I replied right away.

I feel high from last night.

No response.

An hour and a half passed, and still nobody had come to my open house. Maybe if this job required more brain activity, I wouldn't fall down a slippery mental slope into kooky town. I never get this way about men. I don't pursue. Or that was the way it used to be.

The buzzer rang and jolted me out of my convulsing, self-absorbed delirium. I jumped up and straightened my skirt, wiped the saliva from the corner of my mouth, and matted my hair back into place. I had a wrinkle from the edge of the pillow being pressed against my face for the last hour. I buzzed the visitor in and instructed him over the intercom to come up one flight of stairs.

"Is this an open house?" The guy slowly opened the door, looking past me.

"Yes, it's an open house. I'm open a few more minutes." I was annoyed by his question since he had buzzed to gain entry under a printed sign that said, "Open House." There was a sign outside the unit with a flyer that had my picture on it with the hours of the open house. I also had an open house flyer taped to the front door of the unit. Yes, it's a fucking open house.

He pushed his fat foot slowly inside the door opening. He was wearing Birkenstocks. He had feathered dark hair, stood about 5'8", and was dressed like an American tourist but obviously foreign, though I did not ask where from. He was wearing cargo shorts and a casual sport-type preppy golf shirt. He seemed odd, but most tech dudes seemed that way to me, and I just assumed he was a tech dude. I do automatically profile visitors at my open houses, but it's so that I can sell them the place, not consciously discriminate against them.

"Come on in," I said, forcing a flyer into his hand so that I didn't have to shake it. I really am generally able to be moderately friendly but I think shaking hands at open houses is unnecessary and disgusting. I immediately decided that he was just somebody curious or without something better to do and so I sat back down on the couch. I had already exhausted myself with all my inner struggles over Nate.

"I forgot it was Sunday!" he said in a jolly manner. His eyes wandered all over, first to the floor, then the patio, then to my thighs. I was not wearing stockings. He glanced at my legs right where the skirt ended, above the knees. That is a red flag—not something buyers do and not something a strange man would do if he wanted to be sure I didn't feel threatened by being alone with him. I watched his hairy legs as he headed past me to the patio. He pushed the heavy door open and stepped outside, even though any person could see the entirety of the patio and the lack of a view from inside the unit. He looked at the patio next door, maybe into their unit. He seemed like he was checking if anybody else was around. I held my phone as though it was a brick that I was going to have to smash into his nose.

"Did you see it online…?" I knew he was no buyer but I couldn't ask him what he was doing there without sounding rude.

He came back in. "No, I was going to the Hall of Justice but I forgot it was Sunday," he said, without really telling me enough about who he was or why he was here, the only visitor to my two-hour open house for a property in an alley near the jail. "Mind if I look upstairs?"

"It's an open house." I wasn't being friendly but I didn't think the guy would even notice. He seemed to be the type of person who tends to miss some social cues or is too directed by their own agenda to show themselves to be considerate. I did not move from my seat, partly because I didn't want to offer him the opportunity to glance at any additional angles of my body. He seemed to be poor at hiding from me that he was doing that. The upstairs was just an open loft platform, so there wasn't a whole lot to investigate; still, he lingered up there for what seemed like a very long three minutes. I was planning to close up in another ten minutes and I figured if he was still lurking around by then, I would just start stomping around and turning lights off. But for now, I stayed on the sofa.

"How's the market?" *Oh god, not that question.*

"It depends. Which part of the market?"

The guy came downstairs and sat himself down with a clunk in the chair across from me, making himself at home, placing his right ankle just above his left knee, leaving a

gaping space between his shorts and his flesh. I did not want
to see what was inside his shorts. He glanced at my leg again,
in the same spot, just below where the material of the skirt
ended. He looked out toward the patio again, a longer look,
and I definitely had the feeling this time that he was checking
for witnesses. I wasn't sure how hard I was going to have to
fight this guy or if I was going to have to submit.

"Would you want to go out with me sometime?"

"On a date?" I asked, incredulous.

"Yes, on a date."

"You're married!" I scolded him, pointing to his finger.
"You're wearing a ring!" I had noticed it earlier while glancing
at his awful attire. It was one of those Celtic braid rings and it
made me think of post-hippie white people from Oregon.

"Oh, that—we're not really together," he said quickly, dis-
missively. It sounded like bullshit.

"Oh, right!" I will sleep with practically anyone, except perhaps creepy-acting guys with Birkenstocks, cargo shorts, and
bouffant hairdos. But I really dislike being hit on while I am
trying to sell real estate. I think it's rude.

"Have you had many visitors today?" I guessed that he was
changing the subject because I had busted him so badly.

"No!" I didn't need to shout that part but I was alarmed,
and everything seemed to be coming out at the same inten-
sity level.

The buzzer rang—thankfully, another visitor to my poorly
attended open house. It turned out to be a pathetically nice,
older rental agent who was trying to drum up business. He
stayed with me as I closed up the place, helping me with the
lights and chatting with me as I put everything in its place
and packed up my things. Birkenstock didn't pick up on the
whole situation: that I felt weirded out by him and that the
old guy was sticking around to protect me. Birkenstock just
tagged along like we were all just normal people doing normal things, not strangers making themselves at home at an
open house where the real estate lady is totally alone with
nobody to hear her scream. Birkenstock guy left once we all

hit the sidewalk. I profusely thanked my new friend, and he told me he thought that maybe there had been something odd going on. I promised that I would give him all my future rental referral business and I entered his contact information into my phone.

Chapter 13

The Fog of the Trauma Bond

ON MONDAY AT 5:30 PM, TWO DAYS AFTER MY DATE with Nate, I was driving around the Polk Street area, dodging zombies crossing against the light. I was hanging around near Nate's place in case he happened to call. I was hoping he would invite me over but I knew he was working and I didn't want to contact him again and risk his wrath. We had been chatting on and off since then, and he had said that we should hang out again. I kept driving around the block, uncertain if I should go in somewhere or just pull over and sit in my car for a bit. Aimless.

There was some guy with matted hair walking in a circle on the sidewalk at the corner of Polk and California. I think he was putting an orange into the opening of a drain, and he kept circling the drain, then stepping up to it suddenly and stomping on the orange while shouting and gesticulating with his hands like a bandleader. I've heard that lots of those drains are missing their covers because they are made of copper that people sell for scrap. *I wonder if they can really find somebody to buy that stuff or if they just think that's an actual idea because their brains are so scrambled by drug use.*

I was stalling until the afternoon in case Nate finally decided that he wanted to see me tonight. Should I stop at a café and enjoy a coffee? Should I go ahead and eat somewhere or

should I offer to get something with Nate? I knew I was still trying to get a high from my infatuation and I should cool it but
I didn't want to. I felt unhinged. I broke down and texted him
and tried to sound casual about the suggestion that we hang
out. He was mostly unresponsive but eventually agreed that
I could stop by his condo. Finally! I felt triumphant in my persistence and my willingness to be vulnerable about wanting to
see him.

When I arrived at his place, he seemed disinterested in
my being there, barely welcoming. I stood in his tiny foyer,
unsure whether to put down my purse or take off my jacket.
I don't know this person. I gingerly removed my shoes and
continued to stand in the area by the door. Unlike last time,
he didn't really greet me but rather jumped up to let me in,
then went right back to his dark little den where he worked all
day, remaining focused on his phone.

I peered into his kitchen, a cubicle really, barely the size
of two coat closets. The last time I was here, I had been
impressed by the décor, but maybe due to it being earlier in
the day this time, I started to notice the seedy details of his tiny
kitchen: crumbs all over the floor, a dirty little bunched up
carpet, a decrepit electric stove that was caked with hardened
residue, and a vent hood cover that was absolutely thick with
dirty grease. Rumpled black linen curtains hung unevenly
over the aluminum-frame window at the end of the kitchen,
and on the dirty windowsill sat a mangy, ravaged basil plant
next to a grease-covered, broken-looking hookah that was
probably scored at a flea market. To the left of the window,
the tiny counter was covered with what looked like odds and
ends from a second-hand kitchenware sale—blackened trays,
dented baking pans, dusty measuring cups, and grungy hand
towels, all stacked precariously in the small space. The cabi-
nets looked original, from the 1920s, with grease and marks
and chips and stains all over them. His place was dirty, clut-
tered, and disorganized, but certainly utilized, like the home
of a mad scientist. Somehow, I had missed the details of the
absolute squalor of his kitchen the last time I visited.

He was absorbed in his work. I gingerly pulled open the freezer and saw stacked bags of frozen Chinese orange chicken, chicken nuggets, some frozen fish sticks, and imitation crab cakes—mostly brown food. I opened the main fridge and saw that it was jam-packed with a casserole dish containing a partially eaten turkey carcass, barely covered with a wisp of saran wrap. The edges of the exposed meat were dark, shriveled, and hardened by the air. There was leftover cooked cabbage in a pot that looked soggy and caused the fridge to stink. Both lower drawers were crammed with cans of beer. It looked like a beer hoarder lived there. Once I closed the door to the fridge, I noticed jars and jars of what looked like homemade pickles. I imagined it could be the kitchen of a drug addict who had unhealthy eating habits, obsessive hobbies, and the accumulation of random, meaningless, but cool-looking objects.

It soon became tiresome to be standing in the kitchen entertaining myself by politely examining his belongings while he was absorbed in his phone.

"Um, should I go? It seems like you have a lot going on."

I think he was on Facebook, which is what made me think that perhaps he had priorities other than interacting in person. I don't spend lots of time on Facebook, so I didn't know how he could be so completely absorbed by it and I was wondering if maybe I shouldn't have come after all. And then he just shouted at me.

"Goddammit, I'm working! I told you I have to work!" he roared.

I was instantly riveted by the truth in every cell of my body: *There is something wrong with this guy.* It was an involuntary response, a white-out, an emotional seizure that transported me to my mother's house. I was a small child in the kitchen being screamed at incessantly about nothing, about dishes, about having standards, about things children have no idea about. I was in my bedroom being verbally and emotionally and spiritually invaded and told that I would never go anywhere with my life. I was a rat in a lab being shocked until my fur fell out, being screamed at incessantly, erratically, with no way to know when the terror would start again—being followed around the house, chased in a car, screamed at through a door, then ignored, then forgotten, with nobody to soothe me or to show me how to soothe myself. *There is no reason to scream at a child that way.*

Time caught up to me in the present, and I was in Nate's foyer next to his dirty bachelor kitchen, trying to be there, trying to do the right thing.

"Uh, I'm going to go," I said shakily. "I don't think you should be talking to me this way." Even then I wanted to take care of him.

"How am I talking to you, *Ruby?* You mean you don't like being criticized?" He made an ugly face. "How do you think I like it?"

"I'm not criticizing you, I'm just, I'm, I was just trying to let you know I was feeling like I wasn't sure you wanted me to be here."

"You're criticizing me!" he bellowed.

"You can't fucking yell at me!" I think because I shouted and swore it shocked him a little, and he paused for a moment.

"I'm not yelling. I'm Italian. That's how we talk."

That was a little funny, and we both laughed, and the tension released a little. He looked at me in such a charming way, like he was wondering if I was going to let him back in again. I was still locked up and rigid, unable to flee, knowing I should not interact with this person more but feeling pity for him at the same time.

"You sure are a hothead."

"That's true." He reached for my hand and held it tenderly, stroking it with his big thumb. The rest of my body remained stiff from the sudden relenting of adrenaline.

"Let's go eat soup." He pulled me toward him, kissing me on the forehead, then on the lips, another wholesome kiss, then embraced me in a big hug. I was still coming down from my fight or flight and I was feeling spacey. I let him lead me along, grateful to be back on the infatuation track. I took

his arm, and we went out into his trendy, bad neighborhood
again, this time to a Vietnamese restaurant. We sat in silence,
though at one point, he almost ate the paper napkin that had
fallen into his soup. I laughed at length, giddy and still coming down from my episode. I was spent and yawning.

We walked back to his place. It was the second date, and
I was the one, again, who had driven twenty miles to see him,
parked my nice car in his bad neighborhood, and walked to
his place without an escort. It had taken me twenty minutes
to find a parking spot, but I did not complain. It was worth it
to me to see this man.

And then I stayed, even though I knew I should excuse
myself. I was afraid he would yell at me no matter what
I did so I just moved forward, one foot in front of the other,
as though on tiptoes, trying not to set off the landmine, trying not to explode the man. I stayed even though I felt sick
with myself for being controlled by my response and uncon-
sciously compelled to take care of him instead of myself. My
mother's brainwashing from childhood captivity. I could iden-
tify the cause, but it wasn't enough to stop the process. *I am a
sleeper cell. I am a foreign agent. I have abandoned myself.*

I stayed the night, uncomfortable, on edge, the way I have
lived most of my life, not knowing there to be any different
experience for me in the world. I figured he wanted me to
stay so that he could have sex with me again; I figured that
was what any man would want, and I tried, but it just didn't
work this time—he lost interest, and I blamed myself. I tried
everything because I wanted to fix it, but he wouldn't help
and he never got turned on. At some point, he just pushed
me off of him, turned over away from me, and went to sleep.

I lay there feeling as though the breath had been knocked
out of me. He started to snore. I knew I wouldn't be able to
sleep beside him, not touching, not being touched, lonely.
A single tear rolled from my right eye. It was a long night.
In the morning, he got up without saying anything and went
right to work on his computer. I got up, deflated, dressed,
and began to head out. How was it that I was so impacted

by a man I didn't even really know? How was it that we both seemed to be transported into past experiences with no awareness of what was happening in reality, in the present, between us?

"Going somewhere?" he sneered.

"Yeah, uh, I'm going home." I felt so rejected and deprived, emotionally impoverished.

"I thought we could go for a hike up in Marin today," he said with a musical intonation, as though he hadn't just been totally cruel to me with the previous sentence. "I have an interview to do up there this afternoon. Would you want to come?" He was working on a book about the history of water use in some small California towns and he was in the research phase.

"Uh, I think I had better go. It seemed like you didn't really want me around last night."

"Whatever. This is getting old. You can see yourself out," he shouted. I left, and he slammed the door behind me so hard that the walls of the hallway shuddered. I cried as I made my way to my car. *I'm too old for this shit.* It had only been three years since I finally retrieved myself from my most recent abusive relationship. Why was I heading so quickly back into another one? But Nate contacted me later that day and was charming and picked me up to go out to the scenic coast of Marin while he did his interview. After, we went for a gentle hike, and he embraced me as we stood by the water. It was chilly, cold, and brisk but beautiful by the bright blue ocean. We looked out onto the water at the mouth of the Bay under the Golden Gate Bridge. He took a picture of us together and spent fifteen minutes editing it on his phone while I sat beside him with nothing to do.

Chapter 14

Grooming in the Lion's Den

TUESDAY, I SPENT A FEW HOURS AT THE OFFICE but I was just killing time. I had nothing real to do other than worry about what was going to happen when I went to see Bryce at his house. I ordered a ride in the afternoon even though my bank account was running on fumes. I knew I needed to save money. *But I can't show up at his house all dirty and sweaty after taking two buses and walking half a mile,* I thought. It's "fake it 'till you make it" in real estate. I didn't know how much longer I could fake it—fifteen years is a stretch. That's a long time to be dying your hair and driving an expensive car and wearing high heels and skirts and stockings everywhere. That's a long time to be trying to change yourself into a person who is cheerful, optimistic, friendly, and happily able to engage in meaningless banter.

As the driver pulled up to the destination address, I noticed that there were perfectly pruned roses along the house, white and pink. I could hear what sounded like some 90s anthempop ballad playing all the way from the street, which struck me as weird since this was Pacific Heights. I wasn't aware that people blasted music in mansion neighborhoods.

It was a cheery, yellow Victorian with only three front steps up to a gracious landing before the heavy wood and glass front door. I peered in but couldn't see anybody, just a statue of a baby elephant, maybe five feet high and six feet long, like a toy from a playground but in stone. The house was charming and had its historical details intact, wainscoting and original gas entry lamps, but was also completely remodeled and modern inside. I thought about how the heating bill was probably enormous. I actually really hated Victorians, an unfortunate quality in a real estate agent trying to sell homes in San Francisco. I also despised the color yellow—too cheerful, yuck. It was making me sick being around so much yellow, lingering on the doorstop waiting to see weird Bryce for a meeting of indeterminate nature while my ears bled from the pop ballad. Plus, I was worn out and sweaty and I had to pee.

I rang the doorbell again and waited. I was a little worried that maybe I got the time wrong or made a mistake about the date. It was more likely that he couldn't hear me from thousands of feet away inside his sprawling mansion. San Francisco mansions are actually very small compared to Florida or Texas mansions. I am usually early or exactly on time, but maybe Bryce was on a different schedule.

I stood there for what seemed like a very long time but was probably only fifty seconds and then knocked weakly at the door, afraid that he'd forgotten his appointment with me, yet also sort of hoping he had forgotten it.

Bryce finally appeared, wearing a blue dress shirt and blue jeans; he easily pulled the heavy door open, gesturing grandly with his arm. "Ruby! You made it. Welcome. Come in."

"Thank you. I was ringing for a while. Is this the right time?"

"You are perfect." He put his arm around my shoulders and steered me to the center of the living area, near a yawning, green, sectional sofa. I felt stiff. His arm around me seemed a little overly familiar but it also was friendly and radiated heat, which suddenly made me realize that I was sweltering. Though the air in his house was cool, I could sense the dam holding back my perspiration starting to break in weird places, like my scalp and behind my knees.

"Can I get you anything? Cappuccino? Herbal tea? Scotch." The last offer just sounded like a statement of fact.

"No, I'm fine, thank you," I replied, dying of thirst as the last molecule of water left my body through my eyeballs. *Why did I just refuse his offer?* I wondered, thinking myself pathetic. I was probably the only human wearing black stockings during a heat wave in June but I hated my fat calves and I never showed my legs in public.

"I'll be right back. Make yourself comfortable." He skipped away in his soft, blue, felt slipper shoes, and I tenderly tried out the couch, hoping not to damage the exquisite sofa material in the event that the sweaty backs of my knees made contact. If that were my couch, it would have corn chip dust and cat hairs all over it, but that sofa looked like it was rarely used. I glanced across the room to the proud staircase against the far wall and saw a photo of two children, perfect-looking like Bryce, children out of a catalog that sells children. They looked like they were immaculately behaved, and it made me wonder what sort of twisted psychology he had to employ to force those kids into such compliance. I finally recognized the vocalist to be Annie Lennox and I squirmed with discomfort; my bladder was practically distended.

"May I use the bathroom?" I called down the hall ineffectively.

It looked to me like there were a couple of stairs that led down to the next level of the house and then a large kitchen with a gargantuan, marble-topped island after that. The kitchen was antique white but had an emerald-green accent wall. I noticed a door with the initials WC on it right before the steps so I waited for a beat, then headed for the room once I felt like Bryce probably had not heard me. After using the bathroom, I washed my hands, opened the door, and found Bryce standing at the opening. I jumped and let out a garbled noise.

"Cheers!" He handed me a glass. I took it, a crystal rocks glass with a heavy bottom, ice, and what smelled like whiskey.

"Seven and seven?"

"Kentucky Mule." He clinked my glass.

"Oh, I don't drink during the day. I get a headache."

"There's almost nothing in it. Just a splash for flavor. To take the edge off." He winked a demented little wink like he was crazy and had sand in his eye, not charming at all.

"Oh, boy, I don't normally day-drink. But…if the occasion calls for it. What is the occasion?" I asked cautiously. Drinking early in the day usually causes me to go to bed very early, like a narcoleptic, sometimes in odd places, such as in the audience of a touring Broadway musical.

"Let's go sit in the living room."

We headed back to the Town and Country couch that I had been sitting on when I first arrived. Bryce made himself comfortable, crossing his legs. He picked out two coasters for us to put our drinks on and proceeded to arrange them so that they were perfectly symmetrical with and equidistant from each other and the edge of the rectangular table. Everything was right angles. I glanced again across the room at the photo of the two obediently smiling children to confirm that everything was still in its correct place in this Victorian mansion. No sign of the wife on the walls, just the trophy children. *How did he afford this place,* I wondered? Did he make all this money himself or did his wife kick in? How successful was this guy? Did he come from money? I must have been exposed to wealthy people as a child, but my family was only ever middle class and barely hanging on to that class and always letting me know that we were just barely hanging on. I also think it was instilled in me at an early age that wealthy people were better than us but that they were also suspect because you have to be ruthless or entitled to be wealthy. I think some of my ancestors would insist, if they were alive today, that to be moral you must give most of your wealth away—that's my legacy and inheritance. That's why I'm taking the bus everywhere.

"Thanks for joining me, Ruby. I was thinking it was about time we got a little better acquainted."

"I'm interested in whatever you are willing to share," I said robotically, unsure of how casual I was supposed to be.

He clinked my glass again, but he didn't drink. He just smiled at me idiotically like Howdy Doody and waited. I sipped from the cocktail made more delicious by the opulence of my surroundings and the impossibility of my ever being able to live at such a level. I stifled a hiccup and drank again. Lime, bourbon, ginger beer, sweet but also strangely salty, with bitterness after. I felt it going straight to my head. *I should have asked for water.* I took a long drink. *I am so thirsty.*

"So…what are we…working on here?" I asked, raising my eyebrows and smiling, trying to indicate that I was able to be fun, which was not the case. I was totally rigid, maybe because I felt like I was auditioning for a role and I could sense that I had no shot in hell at getting the part. I was faking it as I had always been and always would be. I took another sip and felt the sharpness of the ginger and bubbles go to my nose. He glanced down at his shirt and picked an invisible piece of lint off it. He looked immaculate.

"Well, what I want to ask you," he said languidly before pausing. "Is what do you want out of this?" He looked up at me with his piercing eyes, his smile replaced by pursed lips.

What a fucking dork, I thought. *Just keep your mouth shut, and for god's sake, don't be negative,* I ordered internally.

"Uh, what do I want, hmm," I pondered. I really never know because I'm so focused on what I don't want, on everything that's wrong, on how I'm a loser and a failure, on how I should be better, farther along. I'm focused on the idea that successful people are elitists and get special treatment. I knew better than to tell him the whole truth.

"Yes, what do you want, pick a goal, any goal. Let's start with that." He looked down at the sofa, brushed some invisible specks from it, then looked at me abruptly with a hypnotic glare, his eyes like tractor beams. Something in my head clicked, maybe just alcohol, and I realized I saw him in a new light—in a way I have never seen him before: dreamy-high-school-crush-light.

I had always thought of him as Mister Fakey-Fake Forced-Positive-Attitude Sales Dork and entitled, privileged Good Old Boy around the office, but in this instant, I imagined an impossible romantic story: the tanned International GQ guy being chased by the naïve and pudgy American tourist. I finally had a reference point from which to view him, his dark hair perfectly framing his manly brow. His little dimple in his chin. His nose, with those tiny, perfect nostrils. Manicured nails. His face could be a sculpture. I could see through the outline of his pants that he had giant, super-defined, muscular legs like a horse. *I love legs like that.* He was a large man but nicely engineered, like a finely crafted Italian car, not like some lumbering baker or Home Depot employee. In fact, there wasn't anything to dislike about him other than he seemed to be an alien in a human suit, too nice, too rich, too handsome, and I couldn't relate to him in any way.

This is what I've been missing. All I needed was a drink to relax, I told myself. I crossed my legs and put my elbow just above the knee, propping my chin up in my hand, affecting sophistication. I took another long drink, hoping the booze would hurry up and make me the fun person who doesn't care about anything and can just go with the flow. *If he kisses me now, I'll just go with it,* I thought. *He's married, so I'm not going to try to get with him, but if he can't control himself because of me, I won't resist. Maybe he's incredible in bed, and his wife won't sleep with him. That could be so frustrating to be such a talented lover and have no way to express it. I could be his outlet, his muse, his receptacle. It might also be a relief for him to have sex with somebody who doesn't expect him to do anything like pick the kids up or go to their soccer game or meet with the principal or pay for a ten-million-a-year lifestyle. Maybe he'll take me upstairs and teach me about what it feels like to make love in a mansion, what it feels like to never worry about money.* I watched all these thoughts blowing around in the ravaged landscape of my mind like dirty candy wrappers in the suburbs after Halloween. *Stay present,* I ordered. I tried to snap myself out of it and focused on his lips, which seemed straighter and thinner than before. *Ugly*. I watched the saliva on his tongue as he talked, taking inventory of where his lips were wet and where they were dry. He was rambling on about something, but I couldn't pay attention. He was giving me some sort of advice. I didn't understand how somebody who seemed so stupid could be so rich and successful.

"Did I lose you?" He was laughing at me.

"Yes, but I'm back now." I sounded like an automaton.

"Good to know. Ruby, the reason I asked you here today is to give you an opportunity to train with me to go to the next level, and you don't have to say yes but if you do, it's going to require a certain commitment from you."

"Okay, I'm interested. I mean, what does it entail? Prospecting? Accountability? Following up? Business plan?"

"Well, first I wanted to find out more about what's holding you back. Do you know? I mean, you look the part. We all are wondering what the story is. Why aren't you more successful?"

I wanted to disappear. Was he discussing my underwhelming sales performance with other people? I immediately thought of Tom, the owner of the company, talking with Bryce about what a loser I was. They wouldn't ask me why I'm not realizing my potential, I ruminated, if they could ever comprehend what I've been through. My head was suddenly an echo chamber.

"I've had a pretty traumatic childhood, and I guess it is still impacting me…" What am I saying? I didn't want to overwhelm him or myself. Whenever I talk about my traumatic childhood, I want to cry. It's not helpful to recall it, and as soon as I mention it, the listener almost invariably asks, "What kind of trauma?"

I saw a shadow cross his face as though he were being visited by some thought he had seen before. Bryce again looked at me as though I were sad. He reached out and straightened his drink coaster, which was already perfectly arranged on the table. I felt like he was mentally rescinding his offer to me, deciding that I couldn't be helped.

"I mean, of course, I don't tell people about it."

"That's probably a good decision."

He looked disappointed as he adjusted his shirt cuff under his jacket's sleeve. My hopeful feelings died on the vine. It was probably clear to him that I need more help than he could give me, more than he was qualified to give. *Professional* help.

"I'm just telling you because I think it's something I have to resolve if I am going to be successful."

"I'm sure you're right."

I paused as I searched through the astral garbage littered inside my being to find something to drag out to present to Bryce so that he wanted to help me. There's always self-pity and sadness first and foremost just inside my flimsy top layer. I knew he wasn't going to get it, but it was all I had, so I just started spilling. I had held it in for so long.

"Well, I am working on myself, researching, and trying to figure out how to heal from the abusive childhood I had."

"I see." Bryce looked like he was concerned about my mental status, which I empathized with. I thought I saw him sneer ever so slightly, and it made me suddenly regretful and alarmed. I shouldn't have said anything. *I always forget that nobody in real estate wants to know anything "real" about you. I need to shut the fuck up and get over myself and just change into a fake positive-attitude person, just like he's been telling me all along. I doubt he ever had to struggle or get over anything, and he probably had all his money and connections handed to him by his father.*

I realized my head was a total mess and knew instantly that it was the reason I was not as successful as I should be. The moment I had this realization, I looked up, and my eyes met his eyes, and I saw that he knew this very same thing about me. *It's over,* I thought. *This help session is over. I'm a lost cause. He doesn't know what to do with me because I am such a fucking mess.*

I reached to pick up my drink to try to distract myself from the mistake of my disclosure, but it slipped from my hand and tipped over, spilling all over the perfect table, walnut. Expensive. Apparently, I can't hold my booze at all. I panicked, quickly calculating the cost of all the furniture I had probably ruined.

"Shit. Oh my god. Three thousand."

"Twelve," he corrected me, standing up swiftly.

"Oh my god, oh my god." My tongue was fat and sluggish. I sounded like some drunk at the bar and I knew it, but I couldn't change anything. I should have eaten more today but I was trying to save money. I stood up to go for the washroom, but my legs buckled, and I was on my knees in front of the table, my face almost hitting it. I was having trouble making my body work properly. Bryce swooped in with a towel. Nothing hit the carpet, thankfully.

I felt nauseous and started heading for the bathroom, but I was suddenly falling on my face and onto my hands, and I thought I heard somebody laughing. Bryce put his arm around my waist and lifted me to the point where I was standing, though my legs were sort of rubbery. He lifted me a little more, and we skated across the room, my kitten heels dropping off my feet. I giggled, and it quickly became a cackle. It was my laugh that I had heard. I never laugh like that. I should have been embarrassed but I felt too loopy.

Bryce set me down on a large brown sofa in a dimly lit room off the kitchen.

"I'll be right back," he said and disappeared, leaving me in a space that looked like it was originally intended for a maid but had been turned into a study. I was mortified but as soon as I felt it, I forgot and went back to my delirium. I compulsively reached for my phone and started to text my one friend from the office, Angela, to tell her about how embarrassed I was and what a disaster this meeting had become, but I couldn't see straight and I was having trouble getting the phone to work. I accidentally called her on speaker, and it seemed so loud that I panicked and turned the whole phone off. It was probably better left off, I decided. Maybe I fell asleep. I'm not sure how much time passed. It seemed like at least twenty minutes.

"I brought you some water." I heard ice clinking and looked up to see Bryce maneuvering a glass close to my head. "Did you not have enough water today?"

I looked up at him and he held the back of his hand to my forehead. Bryce was, inexplicably, wearing pajamas, silky blue with little red cherries all over them. "You need to take better care of yourself." He pushed the glass of water into my hand. I was grateful and so thirsty. He sat down on a chair in front of the ottoman and crossed his legs at the knee.

"I don't know what happened," I said, sitting up, although I knew I shouldn't have been drinking scotch. I have passed out before in the past for no reason at all, like that one time when I was on the toilet in the middle of the day or that other time when I got up at nine at night after only one glass of red wine and a little nap to get some water.

"Do you want me to call somebody for you?" He sounded irritated and disappointed.

"I'm so sorry. I just think I have really low blood pressure or something."

"It's fine," he said, but the look on his face didn't indicate that he believed it was fine and dandy at all. He leaned in and tapped me on my third eye with the back of his bent index finger, which was an odd move. He smelled great, like fresh linens, Nantucket, country clubs, a high credit score, and never having to do your own laundry. He smelled like secret investment opportunities and inherited wealth. He took both my hands in both of his hands, then slowly pulled me toward him and rested our hands in his lap. "You know what's wrong with you, Ruby? You feel obligated to people and let them run you over, then sit around with a chip on your shoulder." He looked at me smugly.

"Oh. I'm sure you're right," I told him.

"And you're never going to get anywhere in your life if you don't learn to clean up the mess in your mind. I don't think you

even know why you're here." Bryce stood up, took a step sideways towards the door to the hall, looked down at his slippers,
and paused for a moment as though considering his options.

"Remember, Ruby, there are two sides to every story," he
said and disappeared into the recesses of his mansion again,
leaving me alone again in the dimly lit room. I used my
phone to order a car to take me all the way back to Marin.
It arrived within minutes. I scrambled to find my shoes and
quietly closed the giant front door behind me. Angela called
me while I was in the back of the car.

"Ruby, what happened? I tried to call you back, but your
phone was dead, or it was off, and then I had to meet a friend
for dinner and…"

"I was at Bryce's." I was breathless to tell her what had just
happened. She loved a good story.

"Well, what in the *world* were you doing at Bryce's at *this*
hour?" Angela had a little bit of a southern twang and the caring attitude of a good mother.

"I went this afternoon and I had a drink and I had heat
stroke or something weird and possibly passed out. I don't
know what happened!"

"Oh my god, are you okay?" Her concern was always so
comforting to me.

"And I spilled a drink in his mansion and nearly ruined
thousands of dollars' worth of designer furnishings—"

"*That* doesn't sound good."

"No. And then I disclosed too much about my traumatic
past…"

"Now, why in the world would you do that? People like
Bryce don't want to know about your problems!"

"It was so embarrassing."

"Why in the world were you at Bryce's? Was his wife there?"

"I have no idea! Allie set it up for me. I feel like Allie has
been to his house, and Katy too, but I have no idea why.
I think he was going to do some sales training but once he
saw that I'm an emotional mutant, he changed his mind. I'm
a mess."

"Well, we already knew that one."

"Thanks."

"You know that's how girls get positions at the office?"

"No…?"

"Yes, oh you don't know? Bryce always gets the new girls over to his place and takes them for a ride before sticking them in some big agent's office. You're a little old for his tastes. No offense…"

"But he's married."

"Apparently, he takes them back to his house and does them in his den."

"But he's married!"

"Between that and the nights out on the town with the boys, I would say he's not very married."

"What?"

"Oh, and half the time they end up at a strip club. Only with the male agents, of course."

"Wow."

"All on the company dime."

"Wow. I had no idea…"

"*Supposedly,* he does it to those poor girls from behind while wearing his pajamas. Which you know what that means."

"I don't know."

"God Ruby, I thought you knew all this stuff. You really need to have lunch with the agents. Everybody knows Bryce has sex with girls at the office, the ones who think they get some kind of *reward* for being young and pretty. He has sex with them while wearing his *pajamas* from *behind!* He tells them he's going to coach them or do them a favor or give them a referral or something when really he's just there to use them like a tissue and farm them out for some crappy assistant position with some crony friend of his. Of course, it leads nowhere, more like indentured servitude—with benefits! I mean, maybe they get a fat listing out of it, but I wouldn't say it's worth it! *Would you?*" She sounded like she had consumed a drink or two herself. "Bryce only likes to talk about superficial things, as far as I know. He's very surface oriented. Why in the world did you tell him about your personal problems?"

"I just don't know what I'm doing. I mean, I can't be like these people."

"Call me next time before you do something like that!"

"Shoot. I will. I'll call you next time."

I lost the connection after we crossed the entrance to the Golden Gate Bridge and I let my mind wander as I watched the beautiful scenery. Finally, I was almost back in beautiful Marin County. What a waste of a day, I thought, angry with myself for supposing Bryce would ever really offer to help me. *God, I'm so stupid,* I berated myself. *What did you expect when you can already see what has been going on in that stupid office? There's no secret to being a success in this business after all. It's who you know and who you blow.*

IDIDN'T SLEEP WELL BECAUSE OF THE VISIT WITH BRYCE. Obviously, it was my fault for going to his house like a dummy, thinking he was going to coach me or wave a magic wand and turn me into a real estate star who could sell tons of expensive real estate. I never wanted to do this weird job anyway but I was in so deep and not qualified to do anything else besides low-wage work.

It was Wednesday, office meeting day. The room was bright and jam-packed with little folding chairs for the special meeting. Many agents were already shoulder-to-shoulder in the main room by the time I got there. Everyone's head was well-lit by the skylight three stories above. Some of the agents with the private offices off the catwalk had wandered to the edge rather than join the crowded main floor. It was clear that this was not going to be just a regular meeting. Something was happening.

We were milling about on the edges of the room and at the back behind the chairs, making it difficult for anybody to go from one side of the office to the other. Agents were huddled in their little sub-groups based on whether they were snobby or not, huge producers or not. In the front of the room was Tab, though his mother was MIA today. Ugly-Jacket Lady was sitting in the middle of the front row, spine erect, legs crossed, staring straight ahead, completely prim and proper. She's old but always looks like she's stuck in her childhood as the ass-kissing student everybody hates. There was Alice, the sort of nice, pudgy lady wearing a solid gold necklace and head-to-toe name-brand clothes that I quickly estimated to be valued at $3,500. *Jesus, lady,* I thought, *take it easy. You're at an office meeting.*

In the middle of the floor were the wannabes: the assistants, the obedient people, the hopefuls, the newbies, and non-insiders, the people who didn't understand that the whole game is rigged: true believers. The people who thought they were going to "get somewhere" by paying their dues. Katy was there of course, pen in hand, ready to take notes. Next to her was Alexandra, the divorced Russian with pendulous breasts showcased in a skimpy top—hoping to be swept up and married to an oligarch soon, I'm sure, so she wouldn't have to actually do any work in this awful business. There was Erin, the overweight, younger Greek guy whose mother was a plastic-surgery-prone monster agent. Erin always seemed amusing when I talked to him for maybe forty seconds until he would predictably lose interest and leave our conversation in the middle to go chase some younger woman. He should be required to wear a sign that says, "Short Attention Span" to warn people.

I was at the back with the people who do some business but aren't snobs and aren't huge producers or in the know, plus the nobodies, people so nondescript I can't even conjure an image of them in my mind. The one exception among the bland was Angela, my friend who had told me the gossip I hadn't known about Bryce. Angela was a young grandmother from the South who always wore slacks and flats. We were all talking about an email from Tom that went out this morning about how a venture capital, investor-backed, real estate "tech" firm was taking over our company.

"Did you see the email?" she asked me in a hushed and conspiratorial drawl.

"Yes. Awful. I'm not going to stay. I don't want to be at Resplendent Home."

"I don't know. I'm hoping it's going to be okay. I figure I'll just see what happens…"

"No, are you serious? After they've been telling us for months that this company is awful? And now they don't even warn us that they're selling?"

"I know."

"It's a takeover. Hostile." I had no idea what I was talking about.

"I know, it's unbelievable."

"They have to be working to eliminate agents. Like Uber. Uber won't be profitable unless they eliminate drivers! I'm not going to work at the Uber of real estate!"

"I don't know. I'm probably going to see how it goes. I'm hoping it will turn out okay."

"That's what people said when getting on the trains to Auschwitz."

She dismissed me. "Come on, that's a bit much."

The room was getting louder and louder with some agents working the room, going from group to group to poll their colleagues on their opinion, and comparing notes on what they had heard about what was really going on.

I looked at Bryce and I felt sick, violated, humiliated, and bitter, yet determined not to let it interfere with my ability to function at the office. That guy was never going to help me; I was sure of it.

"Meaningful agents!" Bryce looked all smiles and bright-eyed, as usual, but there was a sense of urgency in the room, the agents demanding to know what was going on. "Before we get started, I'd like to say a big congratulations to Allie, our wonderful receptionist, who is moving into sales. She has her first listing at four million, no less, and I'd like it if you'd all support her by touring it on Tuesday. Allie, stand up. Let's have a round of applause for Allie!"

He held his hand out toward her, and she stepped out of the crowd into a small empty spot on the side of the mass of chairs. She looked like she was going to appear in a magic show in Vegas: shiny black pants that looked like stretchy garbage bags, a low-cut white top with ruffles at the collar and wrists, and a sparkly, loose-fitting blazer on top, plus open-toed shoes with red toes that matched her lipstick. The agents applauded, and then murmurs started spreading around the room. Allie was so young, had only been in reception for six months or so, and was now a brand-new agent, so it was a little bit shocking to hear that she already had a massive listing.

Is this how Bryce made the issue of the "sexy" comment go away? I looked at Angela, and she rolled her eyes and mouthed the words, "I told you," to me. I felt a pang of resentment and jealousy; I had gone out on a limb for her, and now she had a fat listing while I was on thin ice.

The chatter in the room seemed to be growing, the focus of the meeting already derailed. Bryce cleared his throat and spoke again. "Quiet please! Let's get started. I know you all have heard a lot about what's going on and you've been talking about it, so I want to be sure you all know: after many hours and days and weeks of negotiations, we are proud to be joining forces with Resplendent Home, the leading new real estate company that is on the cutting edge of technology. Resplendent Home is threatening to really disrupt the old business model, and we have decided to join forces because if there's going to be disruption happening, then we want to be the ones disrupting!" A bunch of agents applauded, even though what he was saying didn't make any sense. *What a crock of shit,* I thought.

"And some of you, many of you, have contacted me about this. And I just want to say thank you for your support."

It was a brave face he was putting on, but he also looked slightly nervous, tense, and red-faced. He was faltering in his speech while trying to go through his PowerPoint presentation. He got to a screen where he had quotes from agents who made supportive comments to him. It was so weird. *Why does he need support if this is such a great opportunity and he's "out in front" of the "disruption"?*

"Tom and I have been in many late-night discussions, and he can't be here today because he's wrapping up important details with the CEO of Resplendent Home, Gilbert Gilligan, and if you haven't seen his speech to Direction Home agents on YouTube, you should really take a look. It will really give you an idea of what this company is about and…"

Blah, blah, blah. I started zoning out, focused more on my indignation than the BS that Bryce was espousing. Everybody in the room was leaning in to hear him, waiting, hoping for him to say something real, but it was no use; it was all just glossed over by Bryce's smarm, as usual.

The meeting was disorganized and messy. I was shocked. *Why this company, Resplendent Home Real Estate?* We all thought the owner hated them. Months ago, when it became clear they had been poaching the top agents from all the firms, including ours, they had taken some of our big agents, and I was happy because they picked the evilest and greediest ones. It was probably a coincidence, but it sure looked like they were assembling a real "Who's Who" of Satan's All-Star Real Estate Agent Lineup, and as soon as I saw that, I was convinced I would never go over to that company. I had beef with so many agents.

After Bryce concluded his presentation/explanation, the agents began asking questions about the "merger."

"How will branding work? Will we need to switch to the new name or do we stay with the old one?"

"Will we get to keep our clients? Will they be taking our clients?"

There was a lot of fear about losing clients, but Bryce promised the room: "Your clients will remain yours."

I didn't understand—what exactly was new about this company if they weren't trying to eradicate the agents and the agent commissions? In my experience, agents really are the worst thing about a real estate transaction, in part because they are so greedy. Maybe if agents were all low-wage workers, they wouldn't give a shit, and selling your house would be like trying to get Comcast to give you HBO again for free—just keep calling until you get somebody sympathetic and intelligent who will handle it for you. Maybe Amazon delivery drivers could also sell houses. The possibilities seemed endless.

I raised my hand, my adrenaline going. He ignored me and answered some other agent's inane question about their personal business. They were worried the merger would interrupt their ability to do transactions. Fuck you, Bryce, I thought.

"We're all working to make this a seamless change," Bryce told them. "All staff is available to work with you. Just talk to Joy or Roger or any of the staff and you will get individual attention."

I glanced around the room. I was three rows behind and two rows to the left of Katy. She seemed mentally distant, glassy-eyed, not too present, her hand on her abdomen. She was a tiny person. She actually looked a little disturbed and upset. *Did Bryce get her pregnant,* I wondered? There was always a slide projected in front of us at the meeting with a regular quote that Bryce loved and emailed to us after every meeting, something about how a person's attitude was the most important part of their success. It made me so angry at that moment to see it again. I found Bryce and his sayings to be so meaningless. Why didn't he ever have anything real to say? Why couldn't he just be honest? How did he get his money? Was it through having a good attitude? Or was he just trying to make us losers feel bad for being unhappy with getting so much less than the chosen few? It was evident to me that it's easy to have a good attitude when you have a history of being successful or having giant deals handed to you on a platter. It's easy to have a good attitude when you are born wealthy, isn't it?

That's the difference between gratitude and attitude. With practice, you can have gratitude for what you have, even if it's just a little. But you can't force the universe to give you gobs of money by parading around with a good attitude. And you can't create a good attitude just by repeating a mantra, not when you have a history of trauma. Not when you have a history of nothing ever working out for you or a history of traumatic events following you around, conjuring themselves from your fingertips and eyes and lips. And to say that you are unlucky and responsible for your own luck because of your fatalistic outlook in life, well, that's abusive, isn't it? Bryce called on me just then and my heart started beating too hard.

"Um, I don't know if you will be able to answer this." I knew what I was asking, but I was trying to seem like I was naïve, stammering out my question. "I don't know how selling a company works, or, I mean, how selling a real estate company works, but—I was wondering—when a business is sold, like a store, you sell the inventory, right? And also, isn't there 'goodwill' with this sale since there is no real inventory? And I was wondering, of what value are we, the agents? Do we represent value at all in the transaction, like goodwill or inventory? Because Resplendent Home Real Estate is still trying to recruit us, and I was wondering why they would be doing that if they are buying the company. Can you tell me what the agents mean in the transaction of this merger?"

Bryce tried to brush it off. "Oh, well, that's a mistake. They just don't know about it. That person interviewing doesn't know about the merger."

"No, they know about it. I said. I told the recruiter about it, and he said the meeting should still take place." I hated it when my heart beat so hard and my adrenaline went crazy, especially when I was speaking in front of a bunch of stupid agents. I was almost trembling from head to toe. Every agent was craning their head to look at me, and some guy at the back, who looked like an undertaker in his dark suit, was asking the lady next to him who I was.

"The answer is: no. The agents don't represent any value in the transaction. So, no. I'll have to contact them about that recruiter. Who else has a question?"

"I asked the guy specifically about the merger, and he did know."

Agents behind me were murmuring to one another because I was confronting Bryce in front of the entire office of agents. I don't think anybody ever calls him on his bullshit, but I didn't feel like I had anything to lose.

"Oh, well, I'm sure they don't know…Suzanne, you had a question?" He pointed at another agent, deflecting any further comment from or discussion with me. Why was he lying? Bryce concluded the meeting, confident as ever. Katy was gone. I didn't see her leave. The agents were lingering in huddles after the meeting as though unsatisfied but unable to put their fingers on the source of their dissatisfaction. I headed out of there. Nobody was saying anything real.

Outside the office, on the street, a homeless guy had taken up residence on the corner with his giant, crusty mattress. I knew he wouldn't last long—Bryce would have him hauled out of there as soon as he heard about it or witnessed it from his window three stories up. A girl stood by the corner of the building, far enough from the homeless guy that his mutterings were mostly not interrupting her call. She looked upset, crying; she had her hand on her abdomen and was talking into the phone and looking at herself in the building's large windows. It was Katy. I walked over to her, but she was on the phone, and I stopped because she was now staring up at the building. I followed her gaze to the third floor where I saw Bryce at the window, also on the phone, looking at Katy. Bryce was shaking his head in what looked to me to be a condescending and judgmental manner. I looked back at Katy, and her face was full of pain. I wanted to ask her if everything was okay and I thought she saw me, but she turned away, deeply focused on her conversation.

Chapter 16
Another Bad Fight with Nate

THINGS WEREN'T GOING SO WELL WITH NATE. The worst fight was on Saturday night. He had invited me to go with him to see his favorite quirky band that I had already seen. I didn't really want to see that band again but I wanted to make him happy, so we went to Berkeley, and the show was fine—I actually enjoyed myself, apart from the boring music. We lingered after the set, and Nate tried to talk to the band. The guitar player saw that we had spotted him. He passed us, warily eyeing Nate. Nate was friendly like a golden retriever, going after the guy until he capitulated and talked to him. I felt embarrassed for Nate because he seemed so desperate for approval from the guy. I tried to act like everything was cool.

"Hey, hey, man. Really great show, really great."

"Oh, yeah, oh hey, how's it going." He looked at me out of the corner of his eye, not sure if he should include me in the greeting. I stayed flat, like cardboard.

"Yeah, I really hoped I was going to be able to make it tonight. I've been playing my twelve-string along with your last album, it's tight! I've been playing a lot since I saw you the last time."

"Oh, yeah, oh, that's cool, man. Good to see you."

"Yeah, I just wanted to say hi and tell you—you guys were

so great. I mean, but that last show, the other venue, is really amazing—such a unique space. I would love to just rent that place out and put on a show and invite everybody I know."

The guy politely listened to Nate talk about his music hopes and dreams even though he was the one who had just played a show. I faced the guy, a toothless smile frozen on my face, nothing to say. I tried to stay at Nate's side like a support animal: obedient, available, at the ready. If I stayed silent and just smiled, he could get the attention he desired without my interruption and couldn't accuse me of having a bad attitude or anything.

"Yeah? Oh, excuse me, one minute, I have to talk to Jerry." He acted like he was going to be right back, but I felt like he was definitely making his escape and I noted that Nate was trying not to look crestfallen. He watched the guy go over and talk to one of his bandmates.

And then, sweet relief! We were in the car, heading home. I realized how stressful it was going anywhere with Nate. Before leaving Berkeley, he decided to stop and buy a soda for the ride home, but there was nowhere to park, and we circled the block more than once. The more difficult it seemed and the more time that elapsed, the more determined he became and the more upset and impatient because, apparently, he wanted to get home as soon as possible.

Without saying so, it also seemed like everything was my fault. I was on the lookout for an available spot so that he couldn't accuse me of not caring or not helping him. I was really just worried that if one hair fell off my head it would trigger a landmine and we would be at war, as usual. When he missed an available parking space, I thought that I was being helpful by pointing it out to him.

"You missed a spot," I said in a deadpan manner. It wasn't accusatory, I swear. I was just narrating the events, and the fact was, he had missed a stupid spot. And then he blew up at me.

"What's your fucking problem, *Ruby?* I didn't miss any *goddamn* spot!" he bellowed.

My eyes immediately went white, and I couldn't see my surroundings. I tried not to become upset and reactionary because I knew it would just contribute to an escalating atomic argument. "You can't talk to me that way. It's not okay." I did stand up for myself.

"You think you can tell me what to do. I do everything for you. I picked you up and took you to a nice show with my friends. I'm a really good boyfriend. I treat you so well, and you're just a fucking spoiled brat who can't shut the fuck up!"

"You can't talk to me this way. I'm not your mother." I was just guessing at the source of his rage, and it did not go over well.

"*Don't you talk about my mother.* You have no right to talk about my mother. My mother is *beautiful.*"

"Get a fucking hold of yourself. I'm not talking about your mother. I'm saying you can't treat me this way. It's like you're not even present. You're in a relationship with somebody else, not me."

"*Don't you fucking talk about my mother!*" he screamed, like an insane person, somebody who would probably never find a good therapist, somebody who believes all their demented and distorted thoughts. It was too much.

"Let me out of the car," I demanded. I expected him to say fine and pull over, but he wouldn't stop. "I'll find my way home. Just get me the fuck out of here. I can't let you treat me this way. *Stop the car.*"

He ignored me and wouldn't stop the car, so I started to open the door slowly, giving him the opportunity to stop even though we were in the left lane of a four-lane road, two lanes in each direction. Berkeley is a university town though where nobody drives fast. I'm pretty sure I could outrun any car that came up behind or beside us. I started to open the door with my right hand, and he grabbed my left arm hard. It hurt.

"Ow!" I yelled. "Get off me! That hurts!"

"You were going to jump out into traffic." He was covering for his bullshit.

"No, I wasn't. I was just opening the door so that you would finally pull over and let me out so that I can get the fuck away from you. You're an abusive dick!"

"I am *not* abusive. *You're* the abusive one. You're calling me names like, "asshole" and "dick"! I grabbed your arm to stop you from jumping into traffic. You were going to jump into moving traffic. You're *unhinged!*"

"Bullshit!"

"Just stay in the car. This is just fucking perfect. I just wanted to have a nice time. I just wanted us to have a nice time. I don't know what I am supposed to do. You just shit all over me. I try to do something nice for you, and you shit all over me." He was starting to lament, seeming like he was the victim, whining. "Why do you treat me this way? *Why* do you treat me this way?"

He started to cry, heaving sobs like an old woman who just learned her child is dead, snot dripping from his nose, shaking, and he then became quiet. It reminded me of my mother. *Pathetic. I don't even think he likes me! He blows up at everybody so he's probably extremely lonely. It's sad, but it's not my responsibility.* He bellowed at me as we drove. It was unbearable. I tried again to not respond.

"Blah blah blah…my friends…blah la blah…can't take you anywhere…fucking unbelievable…blah blah blah…spoiled brat…throw a fit…loser…blah blah," all his regular diatribe talking points. If only I didn't have to listen to his crazy ramblings. "…but you had to throw a fit…just screaming at me… just throwing a fit like a brat…" I was trying not to hear anything he said.

"You're accusing me of everything you're doing." I said it under my breath, my hands still over my ears to drown him out. And that's when I heard him say, clear as day:

"I should drop you off in Richmond to get ass-raped."

We were nearing the exits for Richmond, a place I had never really been but had heard about repeatedly in the news. Based on the scary reporting, it sounded like it was a desolate landscape of hookers and junkies and gangbangers and criminals and people with guns. My heart dropped at hearing this graphic threat of violence that Nate had suggested. He went quiet. Yeah, he finally got to me. He got me good.

"Fuck you." Spittle gathered at the corners of my mouth; I was about to cry. "You're a really sick person."

"I was joking, Ruby. You were screaming at me."

"First of all, that's not a fucking joke. Second, I wasn't screaming. I was trying not to engage, but you just won't tolerate it. I *have* to respond to you. You're sick."

"I'm sorry." He sounded contrite but also satisfied. "I was joking about that. I shouldn't have said that." It was too late.

We exited the freeway close to my apartment. I looked at the chain link fence along the exit lane, forlornly speckled with plastic bags and haggard tropical plants. Behind the fence was a legion of the happily homeless, with free drugs and free food every day, in my neighborhood. I wondered, how do we humans break free of our unhealthy patterns? First, we have to want to, I supposed, gearing up for my battle, trying to reinforce my will. The road curved, and I was a little closer to my place. Darkness was still all around my ears. Darkness was inside me. I felt exhausted. He pulled up to my building, and I got out silently and ran up the stairs, into the building, up the elevator, and into my condo. Once inside, I collapsed on the floor, sobbing, the cheap, internet-purchased carpet meeting me.

"Hello, sad person," the ugly carpet said. "I will provide little cushion for you and I will provide no beauty." I heard myself, my inside voice, saying, "I can't live this way anymore." I have to change. *I have to change.* It surprised me that my inside voice was giving me good advice and that I wanted to take it. It was almost like a miracle. Then I had three days of coming down from my PTSD.

Chapter 17

Nothing's Ever Enough for Julie

A WEEK LATER, I FORCED MYSELF TO GO TO A SOCIAL EVENT. When you are single, you just have to say yes to things—I read that somewhere. It was hot and, I drove through the East Bay to get to some Indian Reservation where Julie's friend had reserved the pool area next to the casino for her birthday. It was a funny-looking oasis of a hotel surrounded by a parking lot area ten times the size of the hotel. The young ladies were splayed out on various chairs and towels, sunning themselves. One guy with tattooed forearms was mixing margaritas in the shade. I set myself up on a lounge chair half in the sun.

I watched Julie in her bikini strutting around the shadeless pool in the scorching heat. All that starving herself and barfing up the expensive dinners that other people had paid for had really come to fruition, and now she looked like an undulating, upright serpent. Other women younger than me showcased their more curvaceous bodies while I hid under my droopy clothes.

"Ruby, did you bring your own towel?" Julie pointed to me as all her friends looked up and laughed. I had, in fact, brought my own dingy towel. I didn't know what sort of situation this would be other than a casino hotel swimming pool an hour and a half outside of the Bay Area. One of the

115

women attending had brought a giant swan floaty, and Julie
tried to get onto it without it capsizing; Julie couldn't swim.
It was a fairly shallow pool, but I went to help her, shed-
ding my clothes by the edge and hopping in so that I could
keep it from tipping over and she could get on board. Some
guy already in the pool approached the front and tried to
help steady the thing as well while she got in, his face hidden behind the neck of the plastic creature. The guy rotated
the floaty, causing me to go deeper into the pool, and then
pushed it forward, ramming it into my head as Julie giggled
and the floaty glided on the water. The guy pushed Julie all
around the pool as she draped her lean, lizard body over
the floating toy. She used to be so curvy, slender but with
a normal amount of healthy body fat—that's what I had
always thought. I scrambled out of the pool to wrap myself
in a towel and look for shade, sorry that I had rushed to help
Julie while this man was out there, as he was clearly consumed by his desire to offer up the attention that she sucked
up. It was always dangerous for me whenever Julie had a
suitor around.

I hid under an umbrella slightly away from the rest of the
party, not to be antisocial but because I didn't want to get
skin cancer. All the young women were tanning and drinking. I introduced myself to a couple of people and said hello
to one friend of Julie's who I had met before, a sweet young
woman who was there with her boyfriend. She gave me a
giant margarita to take back to my umbrella. I reclined and
drank while watching Julie frolicking in the pool. The guy
was clearly older than Julie and wearing a wet white shirt,
presumably to hide his dad bod, plus swim trunks. He had
on a bucket hat and aviator glasses. I couldn't tell whether he
was good looking from that distance. At some point, he lifted
Julie off the float toy and held her in his arms. I felt like I was
watching a daddy-daughter festival where adult children get
to recover from childhood abandonment trauma by pretending to be children again. He was completely mesmerized,
entranced by Julie, falling over himself and acting like an old

fool. The guy looked familiar to me; I figured it was because he was such a pathetic stereotype of an older man chasing a younger woman, making an ass of himself when she was clearly using him to reenact the damage her own father did to her years ago. It looked disgusting to me, so I tried not to look but just couldn't stop myself. It wasn't until he brought her to the edge of the pool, set her on the edge, and took his hat and glasses off that I realized what I was looking at.

It was Nate. I choked on my saliva after gasping while attempting to swallow my drink. I recoiled and tried to hide more than I was already hidden on the periphery of the party, out of the action.

How humiliating having to watch Nate act so goofy, so clearly in love with Julie. *Humiliating. And I threw myself at him.* I hadn't really wanted to go to the party to begin with because I was still hurt and upset about the last fight with Nate, but now I really didn't want to be there. I really felt physically hurt by the last fight with Nate, plus I was experiencing withdrawal and then total mortification as a cherry on top. I suddenly needed to be home and started to put some clothes back on, though my suit was wet. All I wanted to do was go home and drink alone. I wanted to flee. Hopefully, I could invisibly escape before anybody noticed that I was about to bawl.

"Hey, girl…are you leaving?" Julie called out to me while tossing her hair and adjusting her tiny bikini top over her minuscule breasts. "We haven't had cake yet." She sashayed over to me and stood beside me and saw the strained look on my face. "Are you upset about something?"

"Why is Nate here." It was an accusation more than a question.

"Oh, I started seeing Nate. I like him! At first, I thought he was old but now I think he's kind of cute!"

I was flabbergasted—she had told me that I should go out with the guy and now she had decided she wanted him and just took him.

"He told me things didn't work out between the two of

you." She smiled at me with that little fake frown face. She was a heartless grifter, I decided. I started feeling heaviness in my chest and I couldn't get a deep breath, and Julie didn't notice, and of course, I didn't say anything. It was too much but I didn't say anything. I noticed her skin looked bad, with lots of little pimples and redness on her cheeks; I wondered if it was from all the barfing.

I started putting my shoes on quickly but didn't get them on fully and tumbled onto the hot concrete, twisting my ankle and scraping the palm of my hand. All the contents of my purse spilled out between us: worn-out lip gloss, a phone charger, a disposable toothbrush with toothpaste built into it, a used plastic toothpick, about twenty quarters, a broken pen, gas station receipts, a losing lottery ticket, a squished pat of butter from a cafe I had put in there just in case I needed extra butter, crumbs, a crumpled receipt for something I don't know what. I felt everybody looking at me, but—*I won't look up; I don't want to see Nate*—though I was sure he was looking at me as well.

"Stay. You like cake don't you? Besides, I want to tell you something!"

I looked at Julie and saw her as ugly and stupid at that moment. I don't know why I had been putting her on such a pedestal for so long, telling her how she was smart, beautiful, nice, and creative, buying her drinks and dinners, being her wing woman. I scooped up my belongings and fixed my shoes and headed to the main building's parking lot so I could get out of there. I stopped at the casino to use a very nice bathroom before my long drive home. I had it to myself at first, but then I heard somebody else enter. I opened the door to the stall and, unfortunately, saw Julie waiting for me by the sinks. She leaned toward me and gave me an awkward hug while I washed my hands, keeping my body facing the sink. She paused for a moment before speaking. I was holding my thoughts in because, ultimately, Julie was still my client and I couldn't just vent at her or tell her that what she did had hurt me. I had to just take it and be of service to her, as always.

"I decided to get my license," Julie said. I let out a sigh.

"Are you becoming a doctor?"

"Real estate."

"Oh. Congrats." I felt and sounded dead. The casino was air-conditioned, and I was wearing a wet bathing suit under my clothes.

"I'm worried about the test."

"Don't worry." I still was conditioned to be nice to her, to help her, for some sick reason.

"I want to work for you."

"What? I don't do enough business to hire anybody."

"What about an assistant?"

"Oh. I don't know. I'm not sure I do enough business to sustain an assistant. I mean, I'm not really sure how it works, but I can look into it…" I wanted to get out of there.

"I'm asking you to be my mentor, Ruby!"

A wave of anger was rising suddenly inside me, but I didn't show it to her. "Why do you want to get into real estate? After I've told you about how horrible it is? I mean, it's not great. I mean, yes, any dummy can do it, but it's so stressful."

"Because I want to, Ruby," she insisted, like a petulant child. She slapped the sink counter with her hand for emphasis and stomped her foot. Julie was tall, like a model. *I wish my legs were that long.*

"Okay, I guess. I think I know how it works. I think I can give you a percentage of my deals and then I take a percentage of yours, but I've never done it—we could work out a scale depending on how many deals you do." *God, why is she doing this? I did three deals because of her and now I'm losing a client as well as creating competition for myself if I share everything with her.* I do tend to be very generous with my time and I like to help people, but Julie was impatient. I was willing to help but I needed to figure out how it would work for both of us, and she wouldn't wait.

She stomped her foot. "Just give me half, Ruby!"

"What? I can't give you half. That's my business, my clients. I have been doing this for fifteen years. I can't just hand

you half of my deals *and* train you *and* help you with your
deals and tell you everything I know. I can't give you all
my connections and clients. It doesn't work like that." Julie
wasn't the smartest person I had ever known but surely she
understood this situation.

"Ruby, you don't get it. I got my license to work with you.
I want to work with you. We can just split everything. I'm
getting my license because of you."

"Jesus, why? This job is awful. I mean, I'll help you, but
you have to bring in deals. You have to add to my business
if you're going to take from me. I guess I could start you at
fifteen percent on the first deal, and we could work our way
up from there."

"Fifteen percent? Are you fucking kidding me? That's
a joke, right?" God, she really just didn't get it. She was
so greedy, taking every available man, and it still wasn't
enough for her.

"Actually, I'm offering you fifteen percent of my deals.
Do you get it? That's extremely generous if you haven't done
anything to contribute to those deals. Then if you bring a deal
in, that's where I would benefit, but it's going to be all my
deals. I think that's how it works, but we need to do some
research. I can talk to my broker about it…"

"God, Ruby, I thought you would help me. You know,
I really only wanted to do this because of you. I can't believe
you would be so greedy and selfish." She stomped off in a
tantrum. I just couldn't believe what an awful day it had been.

It was too much hanging out with her. It made me feel terrible at a level I no longer wanted to tolerate. I was starting to
think that she had really exploited my willingness to be nice.

When I finally got home after my long drive, I found that
she had followed up with a barrage of insulting and abusive
text messages aimed at coercing me to give her my money,
essentially. She called me greedy and selfish for not immediately agreeing to give her fifty percent of my business and
clients and she threatened to go work with one of my com-
petitors, an agent she knew I hated. I worried that, if she went

to work with him, she would tell him compromising things about me. It made me extremely uncomfortable.

In the morning, she started up again: a barrage of new messages as I tried to get ready to head to the office meeting, as I drove to the city, as I walked to the office. Finally, in the lobby by the elevator, I responded:

Julie, stop *contacting me. Good luck making tons of money in the wonderful world of real estate—enjoy being selfish and greedy and acting in your own self-interest at all times—you'll be great at it. By the way, as a new professional in real estate, I really hope you don't talk shit about me to my colleagues.*

She responded right away:

Same.

I blocked her.

Chapter 18

A Very Bad Day at the Office

EDNESDAY WAS A PRETTY BAD DAY. The weekend had been ruined, first of all, because of the incidents involving Julie and Nate. Monday, I found out that a client had bought a home without me (after I went to their boring baby shower and gave them a gift), and Tuesday, I spent all day trying to figure out how to design and send a postcard out using our company's online system—pure hell. By the time Wednesday rolled around and I entered the office lobby to go to the weekly meeting, I was feeling fairly defeated. I looked up and saw Katy outside on the street, waiting at the light to cross, then walking by herself, seeming lost, run over, out of place. She looked like she should be hosting a potluck in Texas with those weird blue slacks she was wearing. Her cheeks were rosy with too much blush, her perky lips pink with lipstick. *So low fashion, so Walmart.* She had on very high heels, and I thought, *bad choice*—it's hard to walk around San Francisco dressed like that, with all the terrible Uber drivers, crumbling infrastructure, human feces, and judgmental socialists everywhere. I give her another year and a half here, at most. I successfully closed the elevator doors before she made it to the building so I wouldn't have to engage in more meaningless elevator banter.

When I got to the main floor of the office, it was way too quiet. I checked my phone to be sure it was Wednesday. There was almost nobody in the office that I could see, just the new receptionist, a short, sort of dowdy young woman with frizzy hair and a very unwelcoming demeanor.

"Hi, are you the new receptionist?"

"No, I'm office staff, I'm just filling in."

"Oh, I see. What happened to the meeting?"

"They moved it to noon."

"Why don't I know about it?"

"I don't know. You should have received an email."

"Nope."

"I'm just passing on the information. Don't get in my face about it." For some reason, this girl didn't like me, and as far as I could recall, we had never met before today.

"I'm not being rude; I'm just telling you that I'm here for the weekly meeting and I most definitely did not receive an email about it."

"And I'm telling you, I don't know what to tell you. Oh, wait. What's your name?"

"Ruby."

"Oh, hold on." She looked through some sticky notes on the reception desk. "Oh, yeah, your email's been turned off."

"What? Why? I have everything going through there. All my clients. I have a client coming to town I need to schedule." I began to panic, and a pit of dread opened up inside my chest. *Why would they turn my email off?* It never occurred to me that they could even do such a thing.

"I just deliver the news."

"But why? That has personal emails as well." *And some are very personal.* Feelings of embarrassment and shame stepped up to join the dread.

"I really can't tell you why. I'm just supposed to tell Bryce you are here." She picked up the reception phone and pressed a button. "Yeah, Ruby showed up." She paused. "Okay. Okay." She hung up and looked at me. "You're going to have to talk to Bryce. He says he can meet in thirty minutes if you want to get a coffee or something while you wait." She had no warmth, no personality, as far as I could tell, a real dry piece of toast.

"What choice do I have?"

"I really couldn't tell you." She shrugged as if she was certain I should already know that I was the cause of any bad fortune in my life.

I made my way to the kitchen behind the main-level lobby and helped myself to a cappuccino. I was remarkably calm for a real estate agent who had just lost access to her email. *How could they just turn it off? Are they expecting me to leave? That's the only reason email gets turned off.* It seemed invasive, a violation of my rights. I needed to check my email about a thousand times a day in case anyone was contacting me to buy or sell a property. I rifled through my memory to see if I had given my work email to any of the weird dudes I had dated. The hot back and forth with Adrian before we hooked up was in there for sure. *Oh, God, they have access to all that.*

I sat in the main lobby on our remarkably uncomfortable sofa with the sun hitting me in the eyes. I put on my sunglasses. My phone rang.

"This is Ruby," I answered.

"Ruby, it's Dave. I'm calling about your postcard."

"Dave. Dave…?"

"You sold us the place in Russian Hill? We just had our second baby. Well, through the surrogate."

"Oh, yes, of course. Sorry, I know quite a few people named Dave. How are you doing? That's awesome." I noted that I felt dead inside. "Congrats on the new addition to your family," I said like a robot. Most ladies would have some emotion in their voice when talking about a baby, but I just couldn't conjure it.

"Yeah, I'm just calling to let you know you can take us off your marketing list." He sounded righteous.

"Oh, okay, too many postcards."

"Postcards, emails, all of it. You can take us off. We already bought a new place and we're going to sell on the

Self2Sell site. They only charge half a point." He sounded so satisfied with himself. I always thought he was weird, over-asserting himself because he was a short, angry dude and his wife was better looking, nicer, and smarter than him. I guess she earned more than he did as well.

"Oh, congrats," I said, noting that the pitch of my voice went up slightly more than it had when I was talking about the baby. "Did you use them when you bought as well?"

Self2Sell was a real rock bottom sort of site, full of bad photos and misinformation. They basically just posted the FSBO (for sale by owner) listing and handled the paperwork as far as I could tell, but the pricing was usually way off due to the seller's inflated impression of their home's worth.

"No, we found the house through friends so we didn't have to pay any agents," he said in what sounded like a vindictive manner to me. Some people really hate agents because of how much money we charge.

"Sure, I can take you off my lists. I totally get it. I hate those commissions too." I still had to make a last pitch, even though this guy seemed so happy to not be dealing with me to transact. "Well, if you aren't able to get the price you want, I'm sure I can do a great job for you. I can probably give you back a bit of the commission as well, though it's best to offer a full commission to the buyer's agent." He ignored my pitch. *Nothing is worse than discounting, except maybe offering to discount and still losing the business.*

"I just called to make that request. Thanks." He hung up without saying goodbye, and I felt like a real parasite. He and his wife were both relatively good-looking young people making a killing working for the tech giants. I had no idea what they did but I knew it could not have been anything too interesting and I doubted they were contributing to society on a greater scale. They were just working to consume and creating more humans to join them in their consumption. Whatever. Still, it was two large deals I just lost, that's how I saw it. It made me feel bad.

I watched as Charlene exited her office and waddled to reception. She leaned in toward the young woman, and they talked in hushed tones for a bit. Charlene tucked a folder under her arm, came back to her office, and locked the glass door at the bottom. Then she waddled back to the reception area and called the elevators. I could hear scritch, scritch as she walked, as the fat insides of her thighs and stretchy pants material scraped. I sat there for another long fifteen minutes, certain I was getting skin cancer from the skylights. I don't know why they put the sofas directly in the sun. Every disgusting dust particle was visible on the surface of these sofas, every hair, every piece of dander, every sour cream stain. *Real estate agents are so gross, so voracious, ravenous, greedy, hungry,* I thought. *There aren't enough descriptive words to describe how aggressively hungry they are, both literally and figuratively.*

The temporary receptionist said something without looking at me. I couldn't really hear her because she was looking down at something on the desk while she spoke. I guess she couldn't be bothered to even look in my direction.

"Are you going?" I wasn't even sure if she was talking to me so I just kept my mouth shut. "Hello? I'm talking to you." This time she lifted her head a bit while she spoke, so the sound actually reached me.

"Oh, are you talking to me?"

"Yeah, I said your name, didn't I?"

"Oh, okay, I just wasn't sure you were talking to me.""You going to head down there or what?" I stood up tentatively, certain that anything I said or did would cause this person to dislike me.

"Oh, sorry, where? Where am I supposed to go? Sorry, did I miss something?" She rolled her eyes. I guessed she hated my ineffectual doormat demeanor.

"They've been waiting for you on the mezzanine level for like ten minutes already."

"Oh, sorry, did I know that?" I was completely polite with her, hesitant, mainly because I was afraid of her and could tell that she hated me. For some reason, my hesitancy was like an accusation for her or like a trigger or something.

"Right, like I didn't already tell you."

"I actually did not hear you. Don't get angry." I walked over to her but stood back a good five feet from the desk.

"Not everything's about you, lady. If you walk around expecting people to fawn over you."

"Is that a question?"

"Why, I don't speak English good enough for you?"

"Is everything okay?" I was getting really angry but still trying to be polite.

"Coming from an entitled, rich lady."

"I think you're talking to somebody who's not here right now. Somebody in a different universe."

"No wonder they turned your email off." She was really just raging at me. I walked to the elevator and pressed the call button so that I could get out of there before I snapped. I can only be polite for so long before I explode like a ticking time bomb. The elevator was already on the main level, so the doors opened right away, and I got in to go to the lower level where Bryce was supposed to be.

"Rude," she muttered as the doors were closing.

"I can hear you!" I was shaking with anger by the time the doors closed, and my mind was racing. *Awful!* I was trembling and couldn't calm myself down. I got out of the elevator, walked right up to the glass-enclosed conference room, and immediately locked in with dead-eyed Charlene. A jolt riveted my body, and I started to go back to the elevator, thinking I was in the wrong place. But then a hulking body in a blue blazer facing her turned, and I saw that it was Bryce. Somebody pushed past me and went to sit beside Charlene. It was Allie, her breasts heaving out of her top and jiggling as she walked. She was wearing smelly perfume. *Inappropriate.*

I walked to the opposite end of the conference table so that I could face them all and the length of the table would be a buffer between us. Bryce looked knowingly at the guy next to him: Tom, the owner of the company, an assertive, renegade, maverick-type, sixty-something-year-old-trying-to-act-forty-five business guy. I would call him like, a Lance Armstrong, one of those guys who is super competitive and will do whatever it takes to win. Tom, with his slicked-back hair and his smarmy smile and Don Johnson sports jacket. He was wearing what I assumed were expensive, "casual" relaxed-fit jeans, button-fly too, probably just to torture some woman with long fingernails. With one such manicured finger, Allie pulled her hair from her cheek and tossed it onto her back. As she tossed her hair, Tom glanced at her dangling breasts in his oh-so-casual manner, as though he weren't particularly impressed by bosoms in general and didn't already have a wife and mistress and five children. *What a shitshow.* Charlene remained slouched uselessly like a lump on a log next to Allie.

Tom spoke after an uncomfortable silence. "Ruby, I don't think we've met. I'm Tom." He looked at me, but I kept my eyes on Bryce. I suspected he was behind all of this.

"We've met. I've worked here for three years. We talk at every Christmas party."

"Oh, I guess I don't remember that."

I ignored him and looked at Bryce. "Why has my email been turned off?" Bryce looked at Charlene, and Charlene just looked straight ahead.

"I don't know. Charlene, why has Ruby's email been turned off?"

"Hasn't." She kept her dead eyes locked on me and didn't look at Bryce at all.

"Your email hasn't been turned off, Ruby. I'm not sure why you would think that." Bryce gave me that look that I had seen before, the look that said I was pathetic and there was something wrong with me.

"It's off, clearly. The new receptionist told me it was turned off."

Charlene shifted her lumpy body as some words came out of her. "Nobody turned your email off, Ruby. That's just para-noid. Maybe you should contact IT."

I said nothing and just looked at Charlene with my own dead eyes. It wasn't true and it wasn't helpful.

Tom the owner cleared his throat. "Listen, the reason we have asked you here is that Bryce has relayed to me some disturbing information, and I wanted to be sure we're all on the same page about the rules of conduct at our company."

"I don't know what you're referring to."

"We've had some reports of disturbing behavior on your behalf," he said with an air of authority, though it sure seemed to me that he had no idea what he was talking about.

"Me?" I was astounded.

"First of all, and I should not even have to be saying this, but I don't mind—Bryce is married to his amazing wife, Shauna, as I'm sure you know, and they have two beautiful children together, and we need you to respect that. Bryce can't do his job and be there for his family in the way he needs to if he has to moderate the behavior of his agents."

"What are you talking about? What do you mean 'moderate'?"

"I don't think we need to go into the gory details here in front of everybody." I saw Charlene nodding a little, and I wanted to kick her. "But I think it goes without saying that Bryce deservedly has a solid reputation that he has worked very hard to uphold. And we all need to respect that, okay?"

"Right. And I haven't done anything to harm his reputation." I understood that Bryce had gone on full offense in case I told anybody about what happened at his house. He was a total liar and trying to shut me down before I had a chance to expose him, which I hadn't even tried to do. I wish that I had seen it coming but I don't think that way.

"And we're not here to squabble about exactly what hap-pened and who said what or did what," Tom insisted. "We're here to address what seems to be a pattern of behavior, to address it and bring it out into the open so that it's a safe and comfortable work environment for everybody." Allie whis-pered into his ear, and he nodded. "That's fine. Allie feels more comfortable if she's not present so she's going to go back to her office." Allie skulked out of the room, and I watched

Tom watch her ass as she left. "It has also come to our attention that you have made Allie uncomfortable."

"Wuh-ut?? What are you talking about?" I looked at each of them: dead-eyed dummies. "Bryce was the one making Allie uncomfortable! I went to Charlene about it on her behalf! I was trying to help her!"

Bryce shook his head to demonstrate a denial of my accusation.

"Nobody came to me," Charlene offered.

"Well, I tried to. Because Allie told me that Bryce had harassed her."

"That's not what Allie said to us." Bryce was looking at Tom, and Tom was intentionally not looking back at him but was holding my gaze.

"What? What did Allie say?" I was becoming unhinged.

"I really don't want to get into the details, but something to the extent of you stare at her body, you linger at the front desk for extended periods, and you generally make her feel uncomfortable. Comments about her clothes. I offered to say something to you about it. Allie's not an employee anymore since she's become a top agent but she was at that time, and we can't have our employees being made to feel like they are being harassed."

"That's sick! This is all totally baseless, total bullshit! That's not at all—" I was protesting, but Tom interrupted me.

"And we asked around and we found that it is a pattern." His eyes told me he believed every lie.

"What pattern?"

"Calm down," Charlene intoned judgmentally.

"What are you talking about? I was trying to help her! This is insanity! Why are you coming after me? How am I in some position that needs to be taken down? I don't have any power here!"

"And Charlene has let us know that an agent in the office, a male agent, has added to the information we have about your character."

"What? Who?"

"I'm afraid we can't name that agent, but he's told us that you acted inappropriately via the company email with him as well. He says he has to avoid you and that interactions have been painfully awkward with you since then because of what happened between you two. I'm afraid that we can't share any details because it would no longer be anonymous if we did."

Who were they talking about? Adrian? That's the only person it could have been. Why would he have said that about me? Why are they all trying to take me down? I didn't have any power. I wasn't in a position of influence. What was the point? *Charlene went through my emails!*

"Nobody talked to you. I call bullshit." I stared at Charlene and hoped her heart disease would take her soon.

"They did, actually," Charlene said, head tilted, clearly deriving pleasure from watching me suffer. It was the closest thing to pleasure I had seen so far on her face, ever.

"I don't know what Allie said to you." I addressed Tom, assuming Allie and Tom were sleeping together, assuming that she had said bad things about me.

"All that Allie has said is that you have made her feel uncomfortable. On a number of occasions. And Bryce told us about the incident at his house. And then we have the report from that agent. So, we're going to have to ask you to modify your behavior if you want to stay here. We have some sensitivity training we will be asking you to participate in."

"What was the episode at Bryce's house?"

"That you had been drinking…"

"He gave me that drink!"

Bryce shifted in his seat and finally spoke. "These accusations are just sad. And on top of all these things, and they are not in any way small things, but in addition, we just really feel as though you don't want to be here, Ruby. And that you'd be happier somewhere else."

At last, Bryce had finally said something that was at least half-true.

Chapter 19
Agent on the Edge

I STUMBLED OUT OF THE ELEVATOR SHELLSHOCKED, dumbfounded, mortified, and afraid to encounter the mean receptionist again. I saw her bent over, moving items, or looking for something under the desk, and I backed into the elevator to go up to a different floor before she could turn around and see me. Upstairs, I wandered aimlessly toward the floater station, looking for an ally or a tidbit of reassurance from a kind human but, as usual, found none. Fluffy made a beeline for me, ragged and mangy. I snarled at it and gave it the finger. I was lurching forward, blind, aimless, angry. I didn't know what to do with myself, which wasn't that different from any other day, really, but today I just felt neutered.

Why am I somebody who needs to be neutralized, triangulated, silenced? Humiliated. I heard the lady calling for her dog and doubled back, swelling with rage. I knocked a dog treat off her desk and ground it into the carpet under my heel. I stared at the lady until she shrugged and ducked back behind a cubicle partition. The dog gave me its weird, gummy, trained dog smile before intrepidly proceeding forward to sniff and lick at the crumbled treat. I stifled a sob. Being cruel to an animal meant I had really lost it. *I've been trying for so long, even though I hate it, hate everybody, hate this business.*

I passed an office with glass doors behind which I knew
resided the meanest agents; I could hear them talking about
me in my head, their every past and future derisive semi-
public comment about loser agents taken personally by me.
I was quickly in front of Bryce's office. The lights were off,
but the door wasn't locked, so I pushed inside. I stood at the
coffee table by the entrance, pausing to look at how tidy the
magazines were. Somebody had made sure they were even
straighter and more perfectly arranged than the last time
I had been there. *Stupid. Who cares if magazines are straight?*
I moved them so that they were crooked, then opened one
and crumpled one of the pages, tearing an ad for designer
sweatsuits. I knew if I were a different sort of person, I might
have flipped the table over and kicked a hole in the desk but
I couldn't manage to connect the rage with my body—it was
lost somewhere inside me, roiling and unable to find a vent,
a release, bouncing off my internal organs, pulverizing me
internally, turning my insides to liquid meat.

I had been too nice for too long, wanting too much to be
liked, and the pathway had become too automatic and worn
to go in a different direction. All the other options were overgrown in my mind, thick and thorny with obstructions. It was
too many years of being the way people expected me to be
and too late to change. But you never had a problem before,
I could hear them say, my imaginary audience, wondering
why I had snapped after burning the office down in a blood-
lust of violence, killing all the selfish, mean agents by locking
them in their offices so that the smoke overwhelmed them.
I had always let them do whatever they wanted to me: why
was I suddenly so disagreeable, so upset, they would wonder?

"What happened to her?" they would say about me for at
least the next month before forgetting me entirely, though
I might win a mention at the company Christmas party on
a recurring basis, among the heavy drinkers at least. "She
always struck me as a dark person," they would agree with
glee. "I think she just had a lot of problems if you know what
I mean."

They would roll their eyes and never try to understand
what really happened, never try to do the right thing. And
then they would go back to their stupid lives and positive slo-
gans and entitlement and they would forget about me.

I looked up and saw my crazy eyes in the ornate, gold-
framed mirror on the wall across from me. My roots were
coming in. I looked stressed out, and my stress was aging me
prematurely. I was fat too, not obese, but fat enough to look
dumpy, as in not skinny, as in: I've been deluding myself
all these years, telling myself that I looked "pretty good" or
"not bad," when in reality I had been carrying an extra thirty
pounds drooping on my medium-small frame.

I hated myself. How could I have been lying to myself for
so long? I wasn't as pretty as I had thought or as skinny or
smart or anything, plus now I was too old to even pass for
cute. Now I was in a whole new bucket of the undesirable
and the forgotten. I was just a lost, disconnected person in
the world, unable to make my way but determined to keep
trying: blind, oblivious to the blocks that stood in my way,
the unfairness of the system. They had won. I was a sucker,
trying to get somewhere by being nice, or acting nice anyway, while I seethed in the reality of my failure.

I spun around and looked hard into the eyes of Bryce in
the photograph behind me. What was the secret, I wondered,
hating that I needed to understand this guy: all smiles with
his perfect white teeth and his chinos and docksiders at the
yacht club. He had his arm around Tom, the owner, his best
buddy. Tom looked pleased with himself, wearing the usual
expression, falsely down to earth, barely disguised feral
aggression. Social charm plastered on top of consuming self-
interest. I punched the glass, and it hurt my knuckles but it
didn't break. The picture was securely attached to the concrete wall. I pushed it so that it was crooked, the most I could
manage with my repressed rage and disassociation.

I went to the settee in front of his desk and felt the soft
material. I took my face close to what I thought might be
a bodily fluid stain but as I leaned over, a drop of snot fell

from my nostril onto the sofa. I was crying. I noticed an ugly sculpture: a crystal ball on top of a shiny clear shaft, an award of some sort—best sales performance or best sales captain or best bullshit ever. It was heavy, and I picked it up, knowing my fingerprints and DNA were now everywhere. My first impulse was to break the top off and stab myself in the heart with the remainder, then bleed to death on his velvet settee. He would probably make the cleaning lady take care of it and then release a falsely sad statement about untreated mental illness, causing everybody to commiserate with their fake communal sympathy for ten seconds before returning to the promotion of their own agendas. *I won't give them the pleasure.*

I thought about crashing the ugly thing through the windows, but they were the original leaded panes, and I felt it would be wrong to ruin something that really couldn't be replaced. I struggled with the antique release until the main window tilted open and I leaned out the considerable opening—a person would easily fit through and splatter on the ground below if they were pushed or decided to jump.

"Look out below!" I yelled at the homeless guys splayed out on their dirty mattresses by the corner crosswalk.

"Incoming," one of them called out through his personal fog, though without looking toward me or trying to move.

I looked to the left and right to be sure no pedestrians were coming before dropping the award. It landed with a pleasing crunch sound, and the ball rolled off the top of it, broken from the more phallic part, then dropped off the curb into the gutter inaudibly. I felt a tiny bit of impish glee. I turned back around to face the desk and pulled out the main drawer. There were mostly random office supplies and breath mints, nothing good. I opened the lower right drawer and found some greeting cards with personal messages in them, one signed, "Love, Mom," another signed by Allie, and even one by Katy with a drawing of flowers on it, which I did not read; I didn't care. I threw them out the window and watched a few as they turned and flipped while falling. A couple of the cards landed on

the dirty mattress near the splayed-out men. I moved to the
bookshelf, which had more baseball merchandise than actual
books. The few books on the main shelf were the standard
positive-psychology and leadership books: *1% to Full Boil,
Too Much Pressure Makes Diamonds, Ninja Man USA, Who
Took the Best Banana, 10 Things to Make the Bobsled Better,* and some other incredibly bullshit-titled crap. I reached
to the side of the row of books and pushed them over on the
shelf. Two hardback books fell, hitting the desk and landing
on the floor, but the others just remained knocked over on
the shelf. Why not clean his office while you're here, Ruby?
I admonished myself. Everything I did was just so ineffectual,
so middle of the road, so insignificant. *No wonder I'm such a
fucking failure.*

I heard voices in the hall and I began to panic. At first,
I ducked on hands and knees on the carpet before I realized
it wasn't a winning strategy. I stood up. I had to face the
consequences here. Standing up as though I had a right to be
there would be less suspicious than crawling around on my
hands and knees anyway. I walked briskly to the door and
went out into the hall.

"Hi Ruby," said Gloria, the super high-end agent who
went to all the social events and was always friends with the
mayor's wife or daughter or whoever she needed to be friends
with to get the twenty-five-million-dollar referrals. She was
skinny and bug-eyed from multiple facelifts and made mil-
lions of dollars every year but was so out of shape she could
barely go up a flight of stairs without breathing heavily. I
found her fashion to be garish and her expertise, knowledge,
and service to be on the level of a flight attendant, yet she
was wealthy and successful, and I was not. Who was I to look
down on her or do anything other than grovel at her feet?

"Hi, Ruby," said Genevieve, Gloria's assistant, who was
trailing behind her as they marched down the hall.

"I like your hair," said Gloria in a generous fashion. I had
never heard her compliment me before and I was flustered by
it. I guess I just wanted to be liked after all.

"Oh, thank you, I need to get a touch-up. The roots…"
I started to reach my hand up to my hair but stopped when
I looked into her eyes and saw the slightest twitch in her
almost immobilized Botox face. She was ridiculing me.

I realized I felt sick, almost choking on my upset, nause-
ated with myself for being such a simp, for wanting to be
liked by a legion of assholes, for being naïve for so long, for
playing by the rules, for being a hypocrite and trying to succeed in this world that I viewed as lacking integrity. I felt
ashamed of the accusations leveled against me and of feeling
persecuted, always persecuted, though I did nothing wrong. I
heaved and sobbed as I stumbled out of the lobby and onto
the sidewalk, unsure of where I was going or where my car
was parked. I couldn't stay here. I couldn't stay at this company. I hated Bryce too much to stay. My nose was dripping,
and I wiped it on the back of my hand.

"Don't cry…Katy…Katy… you can have my baby, baby…"
one of the homeless guys sang out while holding the greeting
cards above his head.

"Me too, Katy, Katy Baby," the other guy said as the first
one tossed the cards into the street where they were immediately mangled by the tires of a passing Muni bus.

I should be under those tires, I thought. I felt such terrible
pain but I couldn't locate it in my body. It hurt to move, it hurt
to breathe, it hurt to exist. *I don't want to be in this world any
longer.* I pictured myself stepping out into the traffic. I would
probably feel the hit to my body first, but when my head
made contact, it would be lights out. Would it seem like an
eternity passing between the initial hit and lights out? That was
the question that always gave me pause. It would be slightly
traumatic for the driver, but I bet that he would get a week off
work. *Nobody will miss me.* I cried out loud when I had that
thought, for myself, for my sadness, my sorrow, my pain. *This
life has been such a failure. I'm not special. I can't do anything. I can't overcome anything. There's no place for me in
the world.* I felt so sorry as I sobbed, my body convulsing with
pain. *Help me. I need help! Anybody, anything!*

Cars drove by, pedestrians walked by, nobody stopped. I took a sharp breath in and accidentally choked on my own saliva, sending me into a coughing fit. Nobody cared. Nobody looked at me or wondered what was wrong. If just one person could have expressed a speck of compassion. Nobody reached out. *I'm so alone.* I braced myself on the side of a building, weak from the emotional pain riveting my being. *Maybe I should go somewhere more dramatic like the Golden Gate Bridge,* where the carefree tourists stroll along, and *I'm by the edge wanting to die, wanting to obliterate my consciousness, whatever awaits, whatever is left of me, it must be better than this pain.* They would all ignore me there too—even the cops because my attempt at suicide would be pathetic, ineffectual, *unsuccessful.* I would have to drive there and park and walk and find the right spot and nobody would stop, nobody would care, *which would be so much more suffering,* nobody would try to prevent me from doing it, even if my approach was so obviously protracted, *somebody stop me, does anybody care about anyone,* and they would still all avert their eyes, not seeing the depressed lady head-ing over the rail, wondering where they would go for dinner tonight. Last night was the overpriced cioppino, but that's what you get when you are a tourist and don't know any locals and end up at Fisherman's Wharf. *Selfish. Everyone is so fucking selfish.*

And I was actually saying it out loud now, "Selfish," as spit sloshed around in my mouth and overflowed to the corners while I walked. I was delusional. My body was almost digest-ing itself. In the present, as in my suicidal fantasy, it was the same: nobody noticed, nobody cared. Some guy in a car at the stoplight was looking at me and he actually looked con-cerned. Maybe he just had one of those faces that always looked worried. I knew at that moment I wouldn't go to the Golden Gate Bridge. I would just go to my car and drive home. It was too much effort to do anything else. Just think-ing of it had been like Medieval mental torture, so I certainly wasn't going to try it in reality.

I felt depleted. I could barely walk, barely carry myself
to the crosswalk, to my car. I looked out toward the traffic,
past the homeless guys on the mattress. The horizon was
pink from the fires, fires somewhere in a dusty and dry part
of California. I took a deep, staggering breath that felt like
relief and reprieve from my crying. I forgot about my pain,
distracted by the world around me and the thoughts in my
head. I felt peaceful, emptied, spent. When I got to my car,
I found that the front passenger window had been shattered
even though there had been nothing of value in my car to
take. I drove home along the Embarcadero where the giant
tech company logos were plastered on sculptures outside
high-end office buildings. I passed one that recently had
their CEO ousted with a billion-dollar payoff and a takeover
by its investors. The place looked empty. Floor after floor
had desks pressed against the glass but nobody sitting at
them. I finally spotted one lonely employee at a desk by a
window, slumped over his desk, and thought with some sat-
isfaction, *utopia doesn't work out for everybody.*

Chapter 20
Ketamine

I FELT THE EFFECT OF THE DRUG WASHING THROUGH MY BODY and then my mind, like a warm, pink blanket. *That's probably the blood in my eyelids making everything pink,* I rationalized. I can't even take it easy when I'm tripping. I have to analyze everything, figure out why, what, how. But the Ketamine forced me to let go. I noticed my senses blend. Sounds became visual. My body felt so great. It was beautiful, beautiful. I was not afraid. I didn't care if this stuff blew my mind. It was worth it. I didn't care if I risked losing my memory. *I don't want to remember.* I didn't care if my organs failed or my blood pressure became volcanic. But I was fine. I was better than fine. I felt amazing, pain-free, beautiful, connected.

My physical tension disappeared; I merged with a continuum of consciousness into the blood flowing through me and through the universe. It felt like *I am everything and it's right to feel okay. Oh my god, I am so lucky! It's amazing! I feel so good, and it's so interesting, and I'm learning so much, especially about how there is no meaning after all and I should just chill the fuck out.* I was so high and so gone and then I heard myself say, mentally, "I am everything." It was so loud. *Hello, inner voice.* I opened my eyes and saw the room changing, and it was lovely or beautiful but only because there was no

judgment and it was a new reality. I opened my eyes and
I was aware of the nurse and aware of his awareness. I could
see how his mental energy was affecting the space around
him, reorganizing matter. I had new age-type music playing
in my ears, and it became part of what I was seeing visu-
ally, internally. I didn't feel my body. My emotions and mind
were flowing freely inside the great expanse of my pink body
innards. It was awesome. The nurse was chatty and part of my
trip. It was for a moment intense, and a tear fell out of my eye.
My mind traveled, and I couldn't tell if my consciousness was
separate from the consciousness of other people or whether
all humans living and dead and yet to be born were all on the
same continuum. *Are the living and dead and non-born thinking of me? Are they here with me now?* I wondered about the
nature of consciousness and I thought it was possible that our
consciousness exists everywhere, in everything, in all dimen-
sions of time at once and that it is blended with all consciousness. *It is when I'm on drugs anyway,* I thought, amusing
myself greatly. My brain wanted to figure out the meaning
of everything. It was doing it automatically, reflexively, but
then the Ketamine was stopping the automatic thoughts. I was
working toward understanding something really deep and
then was like, *whatever.* Later it was clear to me that thinking
thoughts and creating meaning are habitual along worn path-
ways in the brain, electric currents of thought, and emotional
seizures with cellular reactions and that many of my thoughts
are not correct. The Ketamine was putting the brakes on the
automatically repeating thoughts and thinking patterns, the
stuck-ness.

The nurse informed me that I could get up, took the needle
out of my arm, and taped a little cotton ball to the cut. I was
woozy. I made my way to the bathroom. I decided it was better if I didn't look in the mirror and I stayed focused on my
sensations. I steadied myself while I crouched over the toilet,
not wanting to touch anything in the bathroom. I was high,
but not too high. The nurse escorted me to the waiting area
and my ride was there. We headed back to San Rafael, and

I spent the rest of the day eating popcorn and resting on my sofa and thinking about trying to work on my mind. The next week I would have the last of the first four infusions. After that, it would be once a month.

Thank God I found my Ketamine. Thank God I have a decent shrink and she got me into this program. I had no idea it was a thing when I went in to see her. I had been telling her that I was going to do MDMA, which I had scored on the street, to try to treat myself.

"Don't you dare," she admonished me. I had deduced that my shrink was probably my age but I imagined she had a normal life: kids, a real profession, family vacations, couples counseling, shared bank accounts. It was just a guess. She was a smart woman, the first decent shrink I've had. She apparently still subscribed to the idea that shrinks and therapists aren't supposed to share details of their own lives, which is something that gets old for me in what's supposed to be a therapeutic relationship.

"Why? I saw the VA is giving it to war veterans with PTSD. I'm sure I have PTSD. I have it from being screamed at incessantly as a child. Screamed at and gaslit and then rejected and abandoned. And so on."

"That's called Complex PTSD."

"Oh wow, that's a thing?"

"I think it's a reasonable assumption that you have CPTSD, Ruby, based on your traumatic childhood. But you're not taking MDMA. You could get Parkinson's." She said it so quickly I felt like maybe she had made up that last part to scare me. I was ready to obey her since I didn't particularly want to use the MDMA that I had scored from the random, weird burner dude who lived on a dirty, tilting boat.

"I have to change myself," I pleaded with her. "I just keep getting in these bad relationships and I feel almost like I am attracting combative situations and altercations with people. And then I end up going back to guys and people who treat me badly. And I can't stand up for myself or advocate for myself. I feel like I need help. I need to change."

"Yes, it can be hard to break our addictions to some kinds of relationships."

I scowled because I felt like she was blaming me for something that I was convinced was involuntary.

"What about if I try to get you into the Ketamine group here?" she asked while looking at her notes.

"Great? What is that?" I didn't know anything about Ketamine.

"Ketamine is a legal drug, used in the past for anesthesia, and this is an off-label use. They're having people try Ketamine for treatment-resistant depression. You get IV infusions, and they are also working on oral options."

"Wow. I never really viewed myself as depressed, though. Just the PTSD. But like really bad PTSD."

"You'll have to go to a Ketamine support group every week. I can try to get you in if you are interested."

"I would do that. I can do that. That would be great," I said, not caring that she saw how desperate I was for help.

"There are guidelines. You'll be drug tested before you start."

"Fine. Okay."

"Marijuana is contraindicated."

"No problem. I hate weed."

"And there are the suggested support guidelines. For instance, Dr. McGillis suggests the need to control the content of your mind."

"Stay off social media."

"Yes, that can be triggering for many people. Also, don't expose yourself to content you are not familiar with that might be unsettling for you."

"What if I'm addicted to being upset?" I was trying to make a joke.

"Exactly. Try to limit that. The doctor suggests that you do proactive things like spend time in nature, meditate, generally."

"I can meditate."

"For the sessions, you'll need a ride there and back—you can't drive for twelve hours after. And the person has to walk you to the front desk and be there to pick you up. You can't just hire a car."

"Slightly problematic, but okay. I'll figure that out."

"There's a service you can hire. They'll walk you to your door after and make sure you get home safe if you need that."

"I see." I couldn't think of a person I wanted to ask or one who might be willing or able to provide such a service for me.

"Other than that, the doctor talks about being in nature, getting enough exercise, getting enough sleep, and avoiding difficult situations."

"Such as every relationship I have ever had and still am in."

"Right. It's about learning how to let go of being addicted to behaviors that hurt us but that we have accepted as normal. Just because you had to learn to accept something abnormal in order to survive doesn't mean you have to continue accepting that pain in your life." I agreed to everything.

"Oh, and practicing gratitude. That supposedly helps a lot. They've done studies about how much it helps."

No problem, I thought. All the conditions were things I was already doing or was willing to do. The only thing missing was the drugs. I started my gratitude right away. Thank you, Doctor, thank you Ketamine. I know it's not going to be easy, but I resolve to change myself.

♋

It has been two months, three weeks, three days, and six intravenous Ketamine treatments since I was referred to the program. The treatments have been amazing, but also a bit of an ordeal each time since I had to pay a stranger to pick me up, drive me there, check me in, pick me up after, and take me home. The whole day is shot, like today, because I'm not allowed to drive all day after a treatment and I am too loopy to go out in public. But I love it.

I felt pretty good when I got home today. Yesterday I was feeling sad and lonely, thinking about how I don't have any family or a partner and how I'm a failure. Those thoughts aren't helpful. I haven't thought about Nate recently, though I did just a little today. I thought about how I haven't even emailed or sent him a text. I haven't called and I haven't returned his mother's canning jars, the ones she told him to please ask me to return.

One of the things we do in our weekly Ketamine group is practice gratitude. I always say I am thankful for my Ketamine.

"Thank you for my treatment. I don't need to keep hanging onto the past. I don't want to be this way any longer. Don't care if I forget everything bad. I don't care if it gets erased and I am oblivious—fine with everything. Blissfully ignorant, medicated, disassociated, obliterated, comatose…my life is not so bad right now. In fact, many times when I lived in flashbacks, there was also nothing wrong with my life. I just have to change my brain so that I can remain in the present." I say something like that each time we meet.

I went to the support group later and I compared notes with the other Ketamine recipients. We scored Ketamine on a scale of one to ten.

"Ketamine for me is a ten," said the pretty young woman who struggles at work with depression and being female and from being from a different culture than the people she works with.

"It's a nine for me,, said the woman whose kids have left and who lives with a husband who now treats her like a child.

"I don't know, I have to say maybe a five. I think I had a bad trip on it last time. I was in the oral clinic and I went into a time warp and I told her the dose was too high," said the older man with the large, black-frame glasses, the guy who loves to shop and has issues with his overbearing, ninety-year-old mother who is so negative that it impacts her gay son's ability to emerge from his depressive periods.

"Have you talked to Dr. Singleton about dosage? Maybe you need to reduce."

"Yes, I talked to her about it. I might have to adjust my other meds. Also, I'm on anti-anxiety and sleeping meds. I can't sleep. I'll contact her again."

"I was thinking we would do a visualization exercise and then a meditation today, would that be okay with the group?"

The nurse often led us in mindfulness exercises that some of us found helpful. I was open to trying anything and I appreciated that this was a different sort of group therapy than the old-style therapy I knew about in which we would talk about our problems until our feelings became all inflamed. What's the point of therapy if you're just going to get upset over and over again about something terrible that happened to you? What if you're a messed up person just because somebody did something shitty to you repeatedly over time? How are you going to solve that by going to therapy when the person who did those things to you is as happy as a clam and flying to Vegas on weekends, going to all-you-can-eat buffets, excelling at their jobs and in society in general, and looking very attractive yet stepping on other people and never working on themselves? They are the ones who need therapy. Or prison. You can't "work through" your feelings about your role as a victim of an (attempted) serial killer, for instance. That would be really fucked up, yet therapists will still somehow encourage you to examine your feelings about it and how you participated. They can't accept that you don't need to talk about your bad feelings toward your rapist or the person who tried to murder you.

The nurse told all of us to think about how we feel when somebody gives us love, and I tried it. Then she said, "Try to imagine that each of us is that person giving love to ourselves."

"That's confusing," I told her.

"I know," she said, "but try."

"Do I imagine that I am me also receiving that love from me as I am also giving it to myself?" I asked her.

"Yes," she said, "try that. But try to focus on that feeling of love and try to focus on the feeling of giving it to yourself."

I found the whole idea very confusing. How am I supposed to be both giving and receiving? If I am giving to myself, then how is that different than just taking or being a black hole of need? She said that her point is that I am giving away all my "nutrients," and, by that, I think she means nurturance, to other people, which leaves me deprived. I guess that makes sense, but the exercise seems too complicated to practice.

After that, she had us listen to a Deepak Chopra meditation, and Deepak's voice said,

"The love you seek is seeking you."

For a moment, I looked inside myself, into my heart, and found only a dark spot. I watched it while I recited the mantra internally and I thought about the dark spot inside me. *Maybe I can pay attention to it instead of feeling sorry for other people with dark spots, like Nate. Maybe with the help of Ketamine, I can liberate myself.*

Chapter 21
An Exercise in Positive Psychology

IT'S BEEN FIVE MONTHS SINCE I STARTED THE KETAMINE PROGRAM. I have graduated from the IV Ketamine to the lozenges that I take at home. I am somewhat erratic about taking them but I guess it works out to be about twice a week. Anyway, my life is so different now. I feel sad for the "me" in the past that had to live that old life. I used to wallow in misery. I was riveted by my conditioning, my trauma. I used to love failure, poverty, and strife. I couldn't do anything right; I wasn't good at anything; I couldn't accomplish anything. I wasn't good enough. I wasn't enough. A failure. A blot on the sun, fruitlessly striving to be a star. I was reactive, a doormat, and a naïf. I kept trying to please everybody but myself and I did so many things that I wasn't okay with, which hurt me. It still hurts. Doing things that you are not okay with is depressing, and I was depressed and hopeless. At my most desperate, I wanted to throw myself in front of a bus or off a bridge.

But everything has changed. I credit the Ketamine. First, it made me see the truth: that thinking is a habit, and how I determine meaning is a habit, which eventually has become an addiction or like an addiction! I couldn't control it—it controlled me, and it made my life so much worse. Second, the Ketamine made my thinking less automatic so that I was able to notice my addictive thoughts and stop engaging them. Third, the Ketamine made my brain a fertile place where I could grow new thoughts and new thought patterns. The brain is like a garden, and I planted new seedlings. It's not immediate, and I have to feed the plants, water them, give them the right amount of light, care for the soil, and so on. I have to watch the plants and not let them be overwatered or overtaken by weeds or strangled to death by some blight. It's a daily thing to keep them healthy and growing in the right direction. Sometimes the plants get wiped out, and I start all over again, and sometimes I get disappointed when I look at my garden and it seems so small and I feel that I am so far behind.

Other things are changing. I'm thin. Not skinny or anything; I never could be completely skinny because my bones are just too big but I'm finally trim. I don't feel like I'm wearing a fat skirt any longer and I don't feel like I need to hide my body or back away from a man so that he can't see my huge ass if I happen to ever have a man in my bed again.

Let me say that differently: I feel so light in my body. I feel unencumbered and free! I feel so young and like a tiny little thing. A baby bird. A duckling in the water. A fawn trying to stand. I'm learning to control and use my body all over again, and it seems so delicate, so new! Slender. I feel limber and I know my relative strength. I am tiny but strong. It's a mantra. I am tiny but strong. I am healthy and fit. It's glorious. I easily do twice the amount of exercise I used to strain to do at all! My old injuries are manageable: my torqued knee, my crumpled spine, my jammed-up hip; they are all stronger now. I am a pinnacle of health. Glory be!

This morning I went out for my little run around the neighborhood, and it was so easy compared to all those years of lumbering around, trying to force myself forward while weighed down by my excess flesh, the flesh that I had gathered around me for protection to stave off strangers and the pain of possible rejection. It was the coat I wore to keep me warm against my reality of aloneness. Now I am glad to be alone—that's a difference.

Another change is that I haven't had sex with any weird strangers or met anybody online or chased after any avoidant exes who shout at me and make me feel terrible and needy. I haven't gone on any vacations during which I have to lock myself in the bathroom while a man rages at me or throws magazines at me and calls me names. I haven't continued to stay friends with or date any disordered people who rage at me in public and to whom I have to say: "I don't want to be raged at" or "Let's take a time out." To celebrate, I took the leftover paint in my storage closet to the dump. I had been holding onto it forever after it was abandoned by that weird painter who lied about why he couldn't finish the job day after day so long ago. It's symbolic: I'm taking out the toxic waste and disposing of it in the proper manner.

Let me say it differently—I am learning how to love normal people. I have a new friend, and she's a single mom who's outgoing and brave and generous and thoughtful and kind. Her name is Rachelle. I don't have any dates or anything but I'm learning how to treat myself well and only have other people in my life who also treat me well. I've come so far! I have friends who are loving, intelligent, kind, and successful. It's such a joy. Some of them have always been there, and some are new, but I'm building a fence to keep out the ones who want to drag me back down to Hell.

I'm making a list every day of the things I am grateful for, even if it's just a ruse. Let's try that again: I'm noting my wins every day so I can get a bit of dopamine to propel me forward. How's that?

By the way, it has occurred to me that the gentlest, kindest, and sweetest people are the ones who bear the scars of this very violent and sometimes sick world. We are the ones who respond, who take it personally when others throw hatred and evil at us. The ones who have no conscience and no empathy are not scarred by the world, or at least not inwardly. They might proudly wear an external scar from their trials and tribulations, but it does not hurt them internally, either because they can't be hurt or they have no internal landscape. One or the other.

Let me put that another way. I am safe. It's so hard to correct the course of the brain, isn't it?

I also want to note that I'm not in financial distress or just barely scraping by any longer. I'm not taking the small amount of money I have saved and gambling it in the stock market until I have lost ninety percent of it. I shouldn't even mention how much of a disaster it used to be because I think that reinforces it in the brain but I do have compassion for myself and for all those failings that I used to be mired in. That part of me felt it had to play small, always be failing in order to receive the small crumbs of what it thought was love but most certainly was not so. That was how we survived childhood, my parts and me, in an unsafe time and place.

Let me start over again. Health is wealth, and vice versa. I know this to be true. As a result, I've hit my net worth goal for the year and I'm now able to build a little rental unit for passive income, pay off all my debt, and invest the rest. I'm able to rent my property part-time too and I can decline any deadbeat hoarder tenant. I can pick and choose only the nicest, prettiest, most mentally and financially stable tenants, non-smokers only. And no creepy guys with a wife socked away in the East Bay renting a commuter flat and looking to fool around on the side. Zero of that type of tenant. Also, I finally figured out how to buy stocks that only go up and pay great dividends, so my passive income is always compounding its basis. I have finally realigned myself to allow abundance and wealth into my life. Also, I can't believe it, but I must be a genius and a psychic because I placed a huge bet on a healthcare stock, a company trying to disrupt the Medicare Advantage system, and it went through the roof! I mean, first, it was in the gutter but then it went to the moon, and I have never seen so much money in my account at once. I know I will have to pay massive taxes on that money, but that's a good problem to have, right? And what all this means is that I can take better care of myself. I can be healthier now if I'm not worried all the time about becoming homeless or being hounded by creditors.

My mind is better. I don't think about Julie any longer, about how greedy she is and how she used me and how I let her do it; I don't hate myself for that anymore. I don't spend too much time hating her for taking Nate and humiliating me in front of her friends or for always putting me down in her sneaky way that sounded like she was being supportive or for giving me bad fashion advice so that I always looked ridiculous compared to her. And I've stopped wasting time fuming about how all those young men always seemed to desire her so much, to push me away to get to her, even though I knew how she really was—that she smelled like old farts and her breath like barf—that she was really just an ugly, greedy, jealous, conniving, aggressively entitled person on the inside. They never saw that when they looked at her and were willing to kill somebody to win her attention or stick their tongue down her throat or parade her around town like a princess. I've stopped thinking about that over and over while wide awake in the middle of the night, teeth clenched, beating out a repetitive rhythm I could not shake from my mind while flexing my leg muscles in a pattern. That's no way to live.

I'm free of Nate too, mostly. He called me a couple of times "just to talk" because Julie dumped him after three months and he was looking to pick back up where we left off. I didn't fall for it. I know I deserve better. Letting go of him is the hardest one for some reason. How can I win with this scenario?

How about this: what can I say about my love life? I met a younger man, and he is so sweet and so handsome. He's earnest and interesting and healthy. I thought it would be awkward since he is younger and so much better looking than me, but he always makes me feel like the more attractive one, that's how secure he is. He works out regularly, gets enough sleep, meditates, drinks tea—you know the drill—talks about his feelings, is good friends with his sister, respects women, etc. He's supportive and helpful and a feminist! He can cook and fix things and is generous. He is really proud of me but pushes me to improve and to challenge myself as well. I can finally say I am at my best in this relationship. And the sex is amazing. Our bodies and minds fit together. We are aligned in how often we want to have sex but if not, if I need a break or feel gross about myself, he's a complete gentleman about it and we are still able to feel intimate with each other. Oh, and by the way, he never treats me like I'm a prostitute and he never tries to do to me any of the weird stuff he sees while watching all the violent and misogynistic porn. I can't believe I have lived so long on this earth without experiencing a relationship like this before. I'm learning to love and trust. It's such a relief and it's only because I've made so much prog-ress in healing myself because I knew I had to do that on my own and not expect my partner to do it for me.

As for selling real estate, I can't give it up because it still pays way too well to forego. But now that I have enough money to survive, I can stop taking those terrible clients and stick with the good ones. No more of the arrogant, know-it-all clients who treat me like a servant and berate me and talk to me like I'm stupid and won't respect my boundaries. No more feeling desperate and afraid to fire those clients who consume my energy and grind me down with months of over-analyzing and rehashing data that I've already provided. Now, I'm able to work with such lovely, intelligent, thoughtful, and capable clients. I feel so lucky!

I know I should not feel joy about the misfortune of oth-ers but I will admit it did make me a little giddy to hear that Bryce suddenly got really fat and looks sloppy all the time. Katy had a baby and moved back to Texas but got divorced when her husband found out it wasn't his. Allie keeps getting giant deals and she's rolling in dough, but I hear everybody says she's a total bitch to work with. I get a little rush of dop-amine when I entertain such updates.

Anyway, that's about all I can come up with for now, Doctor. I understand what you're trying to accomplish with the exer-cise and I honestly think it's a little bit cheesy but I'm really trying to give myself over to it. Like, if I say these things enough times, will my life really change? It's a little hard to believe, after all. Isn't this just magical thinking? I mean, I'm not going to really become thin by being grateful for it in advance, am I? I thought we had established that it doesn't work…but I'm still trying it, so…I wanted to say again, thank you for your help. Thank you for being a part of this program. Thank you for everything you bring in for us to try, the tools like watching your negative thoughts as though they are little leaves floating by on a river. My problem with that is I don't notice my thoughts—I just get activated and I'm in the river already, the river of emotions, and it's hard to see what's on the leaves if you are already standing in the river trying not to get knocked over and drowned. But you said to remember that a part of you is at the same time also not in the river and to lean into that part, and that worked for me. That was how I became defused, not by thinking my way out of it. So, thank you for helping us. Thank you for continuing to have us try these exercises and for bringing these new approaches. I will try anything once. I should have put something in about private jets and worldwide success and everlasting youth and unimaginable riches, plus all the love in the universe. But that would be pure fantasy. I feel like the possible future scenarios I wrote about were at least slightly in the realm of possibility.

On a side note—the refills have been a little difficult to get on time. I know you are busy, and I generally try to notify your office, but then the office seems to be slow about getting the refill notice to the compounding lab. I don't know if it would be possible to get more refills lined up at once? Because otherwise the refill is sometimes a week late, and then I try to hoard it and not take it regularly in case I run out. So, I just wanted to mention that in case it's possible to make it a little smoother so I don't have to worry about running out. I hope you are well. Thank you!

Chapter 22
Rachelle Makes a Contribution

ANG, I WAS ACTUALLY LOOKING FORWARD TO reading this book but now that I see what's in here, I can't even believe I was friends with this person. I'm sorry to interrupt this compelling story and I really am truly glad that Ruby is finally putting her "story" as she sees it out there but I have to say something about Ruby and the way she views herself. And it's crazy what just happened, but I really can't be her friend anymore. We had been best friends for over a year! Our first big fight was when she said she was upset that I didn't get her a discount for the next Ayahuasca session. I told her, "How am I responsible for negotiating a discount for you?" I mean, that's between her and the shaman. I'm not going to tell her what kind of discount I got. It's like when I refer my housecleaner. I don't tell my neighbor what I pay the housecleaner. That's between you and her. What I negotiate is what I pay. You can take care of your own self. And then Ruby said she felt bad about it, and I told her, let me know what you need from me. And, well, I made time for us to talk, and she was all distracted answering the door or something and then she just said she was almost too angry to talk to me! I mean, come on! And she said that she had introduced me to the Ayahuasca people, and that's what really pissed me off. And then I told Ruby she needed to

apologize to me, and she just flat-out blocked me! Unbelievable. I mean, I have this crazy life, and my kid is about to be
expelled from school, and I have this man who is trying to
come over and have sex with me, and I am here taking the
time to reach out to you and try to work this out, and you
go and block me! I'm sorry, but I really just don't have time
for that. I sent her a text just to let her know that she needed
to apologize to me and then all of a sudden, I could tell she
had blocked me! And I'm the one putting all this effort into
trying to resolve this while she's just retreating and withdraw-
ing and cutting me off. I even reached out to her friend, the
one I can't stand because she's so sexual I find it almost
aggressive, doing her exercises in front of us with no under-
wear on! Anyway, I reached out to her and I said, I know
Ruby does this, cuts people off sometimes; I know she does
this with people. Have you heard from her? I mean, I really
wanted Ruby to know that this wasn't something that she can
go say was happening to her! This was something she was
doing. She herself is the one causing all of this. You can't just
run around saying you are a victim all the time. Please. I just
want to stop that narrative if that's what she's trying to put
out there.

I just have this crazy life because of my kids and having
this job and keeping my house running and all. I'm a single
mother. I mean, it's not just running the kids to soccer practice; it's also making sure they are supported and growing as
individuals. And I need to have my own life. I haven't dated
in a while because I really haven't felt good about myself.
I think a big part of that was because my ex, he wouldn't
have sex with me, I would say we didn't have sex for four
years and I put on all this weight. I'm really a different person since the surgery. I had to lose all this weight to be able
to even get the surgery so I did this diabetes drug and also
sometimes Phentermine, which they said I was fine to take
because my EKG came out perfect. I'm younger than Ruby,
by the way. Some people, when they hit middle age, you
can really tell. It's like all the hormones leave their body,

and they look like a wrecked ship. But I'm not there yet. I still have a few good years left and I intend to capitalize on them. So that's why I did this weight loss thing and then the surgery to remove a bunch of stuff I didn't need to be hanging onto any longer and then, I'm always reading self-help books and then like I said, I did this Ayahuasca ceremony with Ruby. I really felt like I connected with this feeling of love when I did it. There was more than that, but yeah, it was helpful.

But this second fight, I just can't even. Not anymore. She said something that was just so mean. I slammed my brakes and told her to get out of the car, then left her on the side of the road at night with her smelly salad bowl and told her, you can get your own ride home. You know, she didn't agree with my telling everybody that she was in menopause and that's why she was taking hormones, but that's the truth. And if she doesn't want to hear that, well, I can only say what the truth is about that. But she got all defensive because she's got this victim identity and then she lashed out at me, saying that she didn't get the Phentermine because she wasn't massively overweight, which of course, was an insult to me. And that was really cruel. It made me want to cry. It was such a personal attack. So no, I don't feel bad about leaving her on the side of the road at night twenty miles from her house. She can get her own ride home. And no, I won't forget that she said, "You are a terrible fucking person, Rachelle," as she was getting out of my car. Who says things like that?

People really need to take ownership of their role in things! I mean, I'm not perfect but I don't walk around saying I'm a victim all the time. I really have been trying to help Ruby look at that in herself, but she can't seem to get there. I mean, that thing with her neighbor's brother was just ridiculous. You go and sleep with a man twice, then when he takes you to a concert and sticks his hand up your dress in front of everybody and touches your vagina, how are you going to say you were assaulted? It's like, it's up to you to tell him not to do that but if you just let that happen, then I don't think you should go around complaining about it. I told her, you need to stop saying it as if you were assaulted, but she had a problem with that too. I don't know. I guess we just see things differently. All I know is I've been through a bunch of shit too and I don't harp on this victim narrative. You really have to learn how to change the narrative. Change your story, that's what I said to her, that's what I do. I have told Ruby that so many times and I thought she understood it. I guess there's a big gap between understanding something intellectually and actually being able to internalize it and implement change. I don't know.

Chapter 23
Ruby's Last Word

THAT'S REALLY JUST UNBELIEVABLE that Rachelle would insert herself into my book. It's my fucking story. And she's trying to rewrite it, to change what happened and change the reason, change the meaning. I mean, that's what she's like, but I have to say it's just totally inappropriate for her to take a chapter in my book. She can go write her own book if she has something to say.

I miss Rachelle. Sometimes. We were best friends for something like a year. But I don't want to be friends with her again. Not ever. Even if she comes to me and acts like nothing happened or we are all good and we can be friends again. Our dynamic was just too messed up. I was fawning codependently with her, doing things I didn't want to do, and making myself available to her when I didn't want to even talk to her or spend time together. I was afraid of her rage. I was afraid of being rejected. Maybe that makes it sound like it was her fault, but it wasn't her fault. It was mine. I wasn't standing up for myself or advocating for myself. I was acting out of fear.

I used to think that I attracted people who violated me: narcissistic people, obnoxious people, and outspoken people. They were so different than me and they could always stand up for themselves. They could always ask for what they

wanted, and if I was with them, I was covered. They would
advocate for both of us, and I wouldn't have to even try.
But inevitably, they would be obnoxious to me and ask for
what they wanted from me, and I could never say no so I felt
victimized. What I see now though is that I'm not attracting
these people to me. They are this way with everyone. I'm
not being targeted by them. *I'm attracted to them.* I'm the
one drawn to them, riveted by their selfishness, their lack
of empathy, their self-absorption. Not that I don't have an
enormous amount of my own self-absorption. I do. The point
I'm making is that I am the one with the problem of being
addicted to people who violate me. I'm creating these situations by seeking out these people who are just not safe for me
to be in relationships with.

I can't be friends with somebody who made me get out
of their car at night holding a dirty salad bowl. I was twenty
miles from home, and she didn't even know if I had my
phone or wallet with me. I could have been attacked or
abducted, and my blood would have been on her hands.
I don't know how she thinks what she did was okay but I'm
sure she is somehow justifying it. I have to remind myself that
I can't be friends with somebody who would do something
like that to me so that I don't ever slip back. It's not okay for
a romantic partner to do something like that, it's not okay for
a parent to do it, and it's not okay for a friend to do it. It's just
not okay.

The thing that was really weird about the whole episode was
that right after it happened, I didn't feel angry at all. I noticed
I felt high. It was the weirdest thing. I seemed to get a high
from being berated and abandoned by the side of the road.

Rachelle is right about one thing anyway. Change is hard.
It's one thing to understand my feelings, thoughts, patterns,
and history intellectually, but it's another thing to actually
change my behavior. I'm still working on it. I'm still working
on myself. I can't believe it's taking so long.

About the Author

Irina Ember is a real estate agent within fifty miles of the San Francisco Bay Area. *Bad Agency* is her first novel.